ALANA B

P9-BJY-457

SERGEANT
URI

outskirts
press

Sergeant Uri
All Rights Reserved.
Copyright © 2020 Alana Baxter
v4.0 r2.0

This is a work of fiction. Names, characters, businesses, places, events, locales, and in-cidents are either the products of the author's imagination or used in a fictitious manner. Any resemblance to actual persons, living or dead, or actual events is purely coincidental.

The opinions expressed in this manuscript are solely the opinions of the author and do not represent the opinions or thoughts of the publisher. The author has represented and war-ranted full ownership and/or legal right to publish all the materials in this book.

This book may not be reproduced, transmitted, or stored in whole or in part by any means, including graphic, electronic, or mechanical without the express written consent of the publisher except in the case of brief quotations embodied in critical articles and reviews.

Outskirts Press, Inc.
http://www.outskirtspress.com

Paperback ISBN: 978-1-9772-2092-9
Hardback ISBN: 978-1-9772-2208-4

Cover Photo © 2020 www.gettyimages.com.. All rights reserved - used with permission.

Outskirts Press and the "OP" logo are trademarks belonging to Outskirts Press, Inc.

PRINTED IN THE UNITED STATES OF AMERICA

Thank You Sarah, John, Lisa, Patrick, Mike, Mom, and Dad.

CHAPTER 1

Sergeant Davida Uri ran around her base making final touch-ups before she received her daily call from the government of Shamayim.

"The world leaders are late," she said as she frantically ran a mop across the floor. "As usual."

She heard her communicator chime and set the mop in a closet. She ran to her communicator to read a notice from the members of the Lucrative International Expeditionary Services (LIES) program. Her eyes shifted to the time the message was sent.

"Two hours late," Uri muttered as she hesitantly opened the message. "Why are they never on time?"

The world leaders will contact you at 8:00 a.m. sharp today.

Be sure to have your mission report ready.

The Government of Shamayim

Uri glanced at the corner of her communicator. She jumped to her feet as she read the time: 7:51 a.m.

She pushed furniture and garbage aside to make her

setup more presentable. She pulled a spray bottle with a scratched-off label from one of the cupboards beneath the sink and cleaned off the counter and table surfaces as her mind wandered off to how she ended up at her base.

Unlike her fellow soldiers, who were allowed to remain holed up in the safety of the barricaded city, Shamayim, Uri was left in the outside areas known as the Wastelands. Her mission was to locate and send any Survivors to Shamayim who had not escape from the mysterious events that occurred ten years ago, when a member of the pre-apocalyptic world's government claimed to have received a distress call from an uncharted location. The world leaders scrambled to locate the distress signal, and within days, every country was affected by what some people described as a virus that caused individuals to lash out at loved ones.

Propaganda spread around the world as a way to encourage all humans to partake in what became known as the Mysterious War. People went into a panic trying to find ways to keep these intruders away from their countries while attempting to maintain peace among their citizens. Some people committed suicide because the humanlike intruders, while others were lynched after accusations of possibly being the intruders.

Eventually, the propaganda failed to convince humans that Earth was winning against these strange intruders. The governments around the world called for an immediate evacuation; all remaining survivors were to leave for the city of Shamayim, where everyone would be "safe." However, half of the population was either wiped out by these intruders or went missing. No one knew if these supposed invaders were a species from a foreign planet or if they dwelled on Earth and had never been discovered. Nevertheless, once they invaded Earth, the humans that did survive escaped for Shamayim and other refugee camps to "live a more carefree life away from those 'intruders,'" as many of the residents of Shamayim called them. Some of the residents described the intruders as looking exactly like human beings.

Uri recalled how she was immediately thrown into a junkyard, which the government decided to rename the Wastelands, right after she joined the marine branch of the LIES military. The government of Shamayim located a group of people referred to as "survivors" and requested volunteers for a search-and-rescue mission. Uri was immediately sent out into the Wastelands as soon as she volunteered.

"It is possibly because you are the only soldier suitable for this mission, Sergeant," World Leader Samuel Gray of the United States had slurred from his office desk over a half-empty bottle of red wine when she asked why soldiers were not being sent out.

Uri told World Leader Gray, "I'm not a sergeant. I haven't even been drafted."

"Now you are," Gray said before falling asleep at his desk, and Uri was asked to leave.

She only remembered fragments of what the world leader said due to the hyena-like laughs on the other side of the wall. She shook the memory away and set up her monitor to call the world leaders. She tapped her fingers on the countertop waiting for her call to go through. The call was declined, and Uri rolled her eyes. "This always happens," she muttered.

She turned her head to face the back of her base and let out a loud gasp.

Her base remained a cluttered museum of bits and pieces from the Wastelands, dishes ranging from paper to glass with week-old grease stains clinging to their surfaces, and dirty and clean laundry piled together along a cracked tile floor coated in a layer of dried mud and sand.

Uri turned back to her monitor with a blank stare on her face. One of the world leaders was answering the call. The monitor displayed someone with his back turned while calling out to someone else at the other end of their office. The receiver stood up and walked away from the monitor. Uri watched as other employees walked back and forth across the monitor completely forgetting about Uri. Eventually, the government's monitor automatically ended the call.

"Okay, Davida," Uri told herself as she walked away from her monitor, "quickly pull yourself together."

She scratched her head, turning around in search of more refuse that had fallen into her dome-like base from the scrapyard.

She paused and ambled over to the old wood-burning stove where a rusted teakettle sat, collecting dust and bacterial life. She checked to make sure it still held the foggy tap water and dumped the water into the sink to wash the dishes.

She let the dishes soak and turned her attention to her piles of laundry. She hurriedly tossed a mix of lights and darks into her washing machine and dryer that were living on a prayer. She felt a rough fabric in one of the piles and dug out her wrinkled uniform jacket.

"Crap," Uri muttered. "I'll be marked down again."

Uri turned to the washing machine and dryer in the corner of her base. She struggled as she crammed one of the piles of dirt-stained clothing into the machine to at least keep it hidden from the world leaders. Uri scanned each bottle of laundry detergent that she was able to salvage from the Wastelands and selected a bottle that was three-quarters full. Its label was completely scratched off with "Unscented" written across the side in permanent marker. She lifted the bottle to her nose and quickly pulled it away.

"Why would I try smelling unscented soap?" Uri asked herself.

She jolted as the notification for the world leaders' call came in. She dumped the liquid in and slammed the lid of the washing machine down. She tossed the bottle into a trash pile on her way to her communicator to accept the call.

As she answered the call, she sat cross-legged on the floor in the least cluttered area and set up the communicator. While the video chat was connecting, her head shot in the direction of the material she needed to present to the world leaders. She jumped up and rushed over to pick it up. She ran back to her monitor and stared at the call menu where a notification for the world leaders' missed call appeared. She swore as she tapped to return the call, and her communicator died because it had not been charged.

"No, no, no!" Uri hissed as she tapped her communicator even harder in an attempt to call the world leaders again. She hurried to plug in her communicator and waited until it turned on again. She quickly entered her passcode and placed the call to the world leaders again.

Uri set her evidence in front of her communicator while she waited for the call to be answered. A screen that said "Connecting" appeared while Uri reached across the table to grab more evidence and bumped her communicator with her elbow.

"Crap!" Uri gasped as she looked down at the words on the screen: "Call ended."

Uri's communicator lit up, showing that the world leaders were returning the call again. Uri swore under her breath as she answered the call once again and prepared for her mission report.

━━━◦((◦))◦━━━

Uri and the world leaders filled the first twenty minutes of her mission report with arguing. She set the objects she had scraped together from the Wastelands in front of her monitor and listened to her leaders respond with scoffs and disapproval, followed by calls for more refills on beverages and food.

Uri held up the first object she wanted to present to the leaders: an empty can with a scratched label that Uri claimed to have been opened recently. The inside of the can contained traces of dried tomato sauce. The world leaders exchanged glances before one asked Uri to move on to the next object without any remarks about the can.

She then brought out a tool box filled with broken equipment. She laid out the contents, including a plastic container filled with miscellaneous nails and hooks, in front of her communicator. She leaned toward her monitor as she eagerly awaited her leaders' approval. The leaders glanced at each other in silence, some even turning their attention toward the servers who ran about refilling glasses and setting out platters of food. Even Uri realized how difficult it would be to prove that she found human life just from discovering an opened can in the middle of the Wastelands.

"Listen, Sergeant Uri," World Leader Gray said, rubbing his forehead with his hand, "we get that you are trying to find survivors, but..." He paused and directed his attention toward a platter filled with strange but colorful concoctions. Gray picked up one that appeared to be pink cotton candy wound tight into a ball. He began pulling off pieces of the delicacy and stuffing them into his mouth.

Uri twitched as she watched the world leaders block out the meeting in favor of the delicacies that were constantly laid out in front of them by the servers, who popped in and out of the meeting room. She could barely make out what the leaders were saying over the clattering of dishes and the loud chewing when they attempted to speak.

"What we're trying to say is that we get that you worked

hard to locate survivors," said World Leader Eiko Himura, who then paused as one of the servers placed a cup of tea in front of her. Uri went to clean off a shelf she missed. She began removing items from the shelf until she heard World Leader Himura take a long sip from her cup and complete her sentence. "However, due to your inefficient...er... progress..."

Uri ran back to her communicator and watched as World Leader Himura helped herself to a strange delicacy that appeared to consist of nothing but rainbow sprinkles connected by caramel candy.

"How am I being inefficient?" Uri asked. "I've been presenting you with clues to locate survivors for a couple of weeks now."

"We've decided to leave you in the Wastelands until you find survivors and actually deliver them to us," a third world leader interrupted as she dumped a couple of tablespoons of sugar into her teacup.

"Deliver the survivors from around the world myself?" Uri hissed. "Alone? What happened to the search-and-rescue team?"

"The team is temporarily unavailable," World Leader Lior Jordan said.

"How will the survivors be transported to Shamayim?" Uri asked.

"Well," World Leader Himura said hesitantly, "regarding transportation, we'll keep in touch via communicators."

"What if the survivors are already dead, or at the very

least wounded?" Uri asked. "Isn't there a rescue team that will be nearby to at least aid them?"

"Sorry, Sergeant," World Leader Jordan replied, "you're currently the only willing volunteer."

"Why is this about volunteering?" Uri hissed. "Why is no one from LIES commanded to take part in a search-and-rescue mission? Or even be randomly selected to participate? Does nobody understand that lives are at stake here?"

The entire room on the monitor went silent as the world leaders exchanged glances. Uri felt her shoulders grow tense while she waited for a response.

A server carrying two steaming cups of coffee immediately stepped into the room, pulling everyone's attention away from Uri. The meeting now slowed to a crawl as the leaders proceeded to place more orders with the servers.

"Well?" Uri shouted.

The world leaders had either muted the call or were not listening to her.

Uri held her hands over her head in frustration and quietly swore as she listened to everyone's muttered "thankyous" toward the server. The third world leader then mixed his desired amount of cream and sugar into his seemingly already sugary drink.

"Well, Sergeant Uri, we had no idea that this would be such a disturbing topic for you," World Leader Gray responded in a mocking tone. "By all means, if you have a better solution, we wish to hear about it."

Heat shot through Uri's body after the world leaders

finished and placed calls for more refills on refreshments.

"It's not that this is a disturbing topic," Uri said. She gritted her teeth in frustration. "I'm merely making a suggestion to complete a task much quicker."

"And you are the quickest and easiest solution for us," World Leader Himura responded. "I mean look at you! You're already in the midst of the Wastelands." She hesitantly focused on Uri's room behind her. "You're really in the midst of the Wastelands, and you've at least presented us with something." She finished with a low, disappointed sigh as she bit into a doughnut covered with sugarcoated gummy candies.

"Can you at least give me more missions that might lead to locations with a better chance of finding survivors as opposed to only letting me travel to scrapyards?" Uri asked.

World Leader Jordan devoured her third helping of cotton candy and tapped her lower lip. "Do you propose that you will cover more ground if we send coordinates of where we might want you to carry out search-and-rescue missions?"

Uri stared at the monitor. *That wasn't at all what I asked for*, she thought. *However, that could work in my favor.*

She quickly realized that having the survivors' estimated locations would at least help her cover more ground than having to guess their locations by depending on the scraps scattered all over the Wastelands.

"It could benefit all of us," Uri said. "The government of Shamayim would not need to be concerned with checking in on me daily, and I could carry out my search-and-rescue missions on my own, which should make the mission move along much faster"—Uri stared at the trays of food attempting to hide her disgust—"since you are all concerned with many other priorities."

The world leaders proceeded to whisper among themselves, nod, and use appropriate gestures almost on cue. Eventually, World Leader Gray wiped a layer of blueberry syrup off of his mouth with a napkin and pulled it away revealing a genuine smile.

"Then it's settled. We'll sync our navigational systems right now."

CHAPTER 2

The meeting ended with hushed "thank-yous" to and from Uri as the world leaders left the meeting room. Uri watched as different documents appeared on her communicator, and she opened each file for review. Most of the files listed disappearances and rumors from the civilians of Shamayim regarding abandoned cities where survivors possibly resided. One document that caught Uri's attention was a grainy image of a small town that appeared completely vacant.

"Sergeant Uri."

Uri looked up at her monitor to see World Leader Jordan holding her index finger on the call button. A few of the other world leaders remained in the room, sipping cups of water as they put away their communicators and proceeded to tap their fingers against the meeting table, waiting on the world leader of Israel.

"We need to give you one last document."

The document appeared on Uri's communicator. She opened it to a news article on the front page with the title and subtitle:

SURVIVORS? WE DON'T THINK SO!

The article covered a failed mission involving a Shamayim search-and-rescue team that came back from the town claiming only to "have been attacked by worms," as the article quoted. Uri scrolled down further to see a picture of the team. All members were covered in scratches and bite marks, and all were frowning. Uri scrolled down to a second article that World Leader Jordan did not show.

"Man or Monster? Strange Shadow Blamed for Disturbing Townspeople"

Uri scanned the article. It explained that before the Mysterious War, the locals believed that the town was haunted by a "shadow" as they collectively decided to call it. The only pictures that accompanied the article was of the town's occupied square shot from a store's rooftop next to a scan of someone's roughly drawn depiction of the shadow in charcoal.

Uri zoomed in and out of the photo of the town. "Where could you be?" she murmured. The photo had a few texture pop-ins, and when those parts of the photo became clear, they only made the shadow more difficult to find.

"Sergeant," World Leader Jordan said.

"I am here," Uri said as she quickly pulled herself out of her trance and minimized the images to focus back on World Leader Jordan.

"Understand that these survivors may not always be too welcoming, and it's possible that they may move on before you're able to reach them," Jordan explained. "So try to approach them as calmly as possible."

Uri nodded as World Leader Jordan turned off her monitor. She then took a joyful sigh of relief before rushing to grab everything she needed for her mission.

As Uri stuffed her backpack with the necessary equipment, she noticed a flash of movement out of the corner of her eye. She turned in the direction of the movement to see a small stack of empty cardboard boxes fall onto the floor.

Uri stared at the boxes to watch for the movement again. When she did not see anything else, she shook her head and returned to packing. She hurried to the sink to fill up a canteen with water. She flinched when she heard the light shuffling of papers coming from the corner of her base. She turned around, accidentally spilling water onto the counter. The shuffling sounded again, and Uri's eyes darted to a corner where a mischief of rats plodded through a pile of trash and along the tile floor, each one communicating through its squeaks.

"Why am I so jumpy? I should be used to that sound by now," Uri said as she turned to close the door. She flinched again when she caught more movement from the corner of her eye. She looked back inside her base and waited. The room remained completely still, with the occasional rat skittering across the floor. Uri shook her head and exited her base.

Auras of heat flowed from the metal as the midmorning sun crawled over the scrapyard. Uri immediately turned her head down to her communicator in response to the blinding sunlight. She leaned her head forward until the

communicator was completely protected by shade, and she pulled up the message with the documents provided by the world leaders.

The only information in the message was the news article regarding the fictional creatures that invaded the town. Uri entered the address of the location on her communicator and followed the communicator's snippy directions.

"Keep walking forward!" the communicator barked. "Turn right, here!"

Uri kept up her brisk walk as her communicator said, "Turn left; in a quarter mile, turn right!"

She listened as her communicator ran through directions until it chimed, "Turn left here; you will arrive at your destination in five hundred feet."

Uri looked up from her communicator to see the pole of a street sign wrapped around a car. It twisted into an arrow leading her to the entrance of a small town approximately ten miles from her base.

"I'm not even sure if anyone is still alive," Uri murmured as she stopped to examine three corpses piled on each other in an alleyway with barely any recognizable features. The corpses were near skeletons rotting inside of a maroon slime that kept them joined at their arms.

The corpse on the bottom of the pile lay across a duffel bag with a tag that read "To the Hawkins's government. Do not lose, and do not report to Shamayim's government."

"Who are the Hawkinses?" Uri asked herself as she knelt down to examine the duffel bag. The bag had been left un-zipped, and some documents covered in dry blood poked out from the opening. Uri carefully pulled back the sides of the bag and quickly backed away. Inside was a bloated brown rat about ten inches long from its head to its tail on top of a pile of red and black leeches. Uri swallowed as one of the leeches let out a humanlike scream in response to her intrusion and bit off a piece of the rat's flesh. Uri quickly slipped her hand beneath the document and pulled it out. The leech let out a sharp screech, and the rat tumbled off of the document and deeper into the bag. Uri caught the sound of glass breaking and looked down to see the leeches wrapping themselves around the containers to brace them-selves from falling. Each one emitted a hissing noise as they squeezed the containers tight enough to break them.

The leeches' red and black gradient skin was coated in the maroon slime that formed a trail behind them as they crawled across the documents.

A greasy stain from the rat's corpse covered the center of the document and smudged some of the words, while some pieces of the document had been nibbled on. Uri could only make out the words "leeches" and "Glass City." Everything else was unreadable.

She felt something slither across her boot. She looked down to see a long, thin, scaly white tail wrap around her ankle. The white tail shifted to a dark green to match the green in Uri's uniform and forcefully yanked on her leg, dragging her toward an alleyway. Uri crashed into a pair of steel trash cans setting off cries similar to those of an elephant in the distance. She looked up to see a ten-foot reptile rise onto one of the houses and crush it beneath its force.

The reptile dived for Uri. She felt the strap on her rifle snap and looked back to see the reptile swallow her rifle in one bite.

Uri backed up into the alleyway and stared at the reptile's composition. It had the head of an iguana, the body and tail of a chameleon, and the feet of a Komodo dragon, as well as a more advanced color change, yet the color of its skin would always revert to white. It turned its head revealing the muscle and bone on its face, as well as an eyeball hanging loosely by a group of optical nerves.

The reptile panted from dehydration and dug deep into the ground until it busted a sewer pipe. It gasped as it lapped up the filthy water spilling out of the hole. It let out another wail and went back to thrashing its body into buildings for a few minutes before returning for another drink from the pipe.

Uri slipped around the town in an attempt to leave without being detected. The reptile twitched, and its head shot up to sniff at the air. Uri rushed to the next building behind her as the reptile looked the other way. Her pant leg caught onto a piece of loose wood, causing it to make a cracking noise. She gasped and looked up. The reptile stopped and turned in Uri's direction, unleashing a loud roar.

"Crap," she murmured.

⟫⟪◉⟫⟪

The reptile then thrashed against buildings, allowing the debris to dig deeper into a wound on its face. It shifted its tail, throwing Uri into a mix of blood and debris. Uri battle-crawled out of the wreckage and sprinted to the other side of the street. She slid behind the first alleyway she came to and watched the reptile in awe and fear.

The reptile shifted its body, and its scales changed to match the color of the dirt. It crawled around the town of Pine's Grove, recklessly whipping its slender tail into the wooden buildings and billboards. It let out another scream and dug through the piles of shredded wood. Uri assumed that the reptile was in a desperate search for any food or

water it could salvage.

Wooden planks and glass shards flew through the air, scraping Uri's flesh. Uri grunted as blood trickled down her arms, carrying the pieces of glass and wood with its current.

Holding back her screams, Uri bit her lip, and picked the glass out of her flesh. She heard the reptile cry again and looked up.

The reptile shifted its ten-foot-long body and buried its face in the ground. It attempted to drag its body through the dirt, creating a trench and causing its sand-colored flesh to change back to a dark red and then to a clear rainbow pattern. It whipped its body around again, revealing the side of its face that was ripped away, before running into another building. It tried running up and onto the side of a two-story building. The reptile scratched its side, and fell back onto the ground. It turned to its right. Uri looked closely to see that it was unable to move efficiently due to its fifth leg, which hung from the joint of its right hind leg.

"Please, don't see me," Uri murmured as she prepared a grenade.

She threw the grenade at the reptile and watched in horror as it bounced off of the reptile's jagged scales and exploded when it hit the ground.

The reptile sniffed at the smoke, and muddled along without any regard for the grenade going off. It crawled to the building Uri hid behind and thrashed its body from side to side, causing the wall to fall and the rest of the building to collapse.

Uri crawled toward a grocery store as she dug through her backpack. She quickly looked back to see the reptile crawl onto the building and the wood crumble beneath its feet like an autumn leaf. The reptile then dragged its stomach across the pile of wood and glass as it moved toward the next building. It cried and slammed the side of its head into the building's storefront. Shards of glass and splinters of wood flew out from beneath the reptile's body and dug into Uri's flesh and clothes.

She dug her teeth into her bottom lip and crawled to the next building. She looked back and saw that the reptile was focused on tearing apart its limp leg. Uri then worked to pluck out the glass without creating any noise. She stopped to watch the blood run from her arms.

"Will the reptile be able to smell me?" she asked herself. She stopped and turned back to watch the beast again.

The reptile dragged its body to the other side, where Uri was hiding. Uri stumbled backward as it turned toward the next house and dug its face into the roof. Shingles flew across the town, breaking the glass windows of storefronts and houses.

Uri rooted through her backpack, unsure about what she could use against the creature.

The reptile coughed up blood and splinters before skittering back to the other side of the street much faster, demolishing more of the nearby buildings.

Uri quickly studied the reptile. She shuddered when she became aware that she needed to give it a more creative name than "the reptilian creature" or simply "the reptile," due to the fact that she needed to simplify the name for her report to the world leaders that evening.

That is, if I return to base in one undigested piece, she thought.

The reptile cried out and slammed its head into a brick building repetitively. Saliva and blood dripped from its mouth onto the walls that came crumbling down. The reptile pulled its head out, spitting out blood and chunks of brick. It screamed again, possibly irritated by its failed attempt to catch Uri.

The reptile proceeded to lap up its blood as it poured onto the ground. Uri stood back and observed as the reptile slowly became cannibalistic. Its flesh turned a cherry red as it turned its head around and sunk its teeth into its limp leg, tearing off the flesh with ease.

It then brought its front leg up and clawed at the scar across its face, pulling off what little muscle was left until it reached the bone. It turned away from where Uri was hiding, and its back curled upward. Then it smothered its face into the ground, roaring as it caked dirt onto its scar.

Uri backed up, surprised at the reptile's unpredictable behavior. "It's killing itself," she whispered.

The reptile then rolled around, stirring up blood and dust as it bumped into one last building and slowly let out its final breath. Uri backed up to watch as the reptile twitched and scratched at the floor. She waited for what felt like hours for the reptile to die.

The reptile squirmed once more before becoming completely limp. Uri took that as a sign to search the travel agency. She squeezed between the lizard and the broken wall, and around the interior of the building. Aside from the blood splatters, there were advertisements for different places around the world.

Uri assumed that the building was once used as a trip advisor's office due to the images and the brochures of various vacation locations littering the room. She looked through the mess until she picked up one brochure advertising a place called "Glass City," showing a collection of buildings that appeared to be constructed of glass glistening underneath a scorching desert sun.

Uri caught the sound of running feet. She looked outside of the travel agency. The buildings creaked with the gentle breeze that ran through the cracks in the wood. When Uri did not see anything, she looked back at the brochure. She tilted it, watching as the city shined in the light, obviously an advertising ploy to make the destination more appealing.

Uri placed the brochure in her backpack along with the samples from the lizard. As she left the travel agency, she heard the feet sprinting back and forth again. She turned back to the town and saw nothing.

"Am I imagining things?" Uri asked herself.

She looked down to see the lizard's corpse twitch against the building. Pieces of wood fell onto the ground, creating a pitter-patter similar to human footsteps. Uri cautiously walked around each of the buildings, searching for the source of the footsteps.

As she went back to picking off samples of the reptile's flesh, the movement continued out of the corner of her eye. She watched the lizard's corpse settle into the building again.

Uri turned to exit the town, listening to the mysterious patter of feet.

CHAPTER 3

Uri came to the gate of the glimmering Shamayim. She perked up as she watched the world leaders approach the gate. The world leader of Israel reached the gate first and slipped her hand through the bars, signaling Uri to come closer. Uri slipped the reptile's DNA samples through the gate and watched eagerly as the world leaders went inside their office building.

Uri looked up to the city as she waited for them to return with a verdict on what she had found. She only lived a couple of miles from Shamayim but knew that the world leaders were often against the idea of them leaving the comfort of the barricaded city.

Uri opened up her communicator to scratch out different names to use for her new discovery if it truly was a new species of reptile. She scratched out over one hundred names on her communicator but kept the name "prism lizard" in mind, due to the many color changes the lizard could make.

Uri's thoughts were broken when she saw the world leaders step out of their office building. They appeared to be talking excitedly with each other at first. Once they reached the gate, their smiles faded. The world leader of the United States was the first to step forward and announce firmly, "The data you have provided us has been denied. We will send you another set of directions that should direct you to survivors."

The world leaders abruptly turned their backs to Uri and headed back to their office building.

"Hold on!" Uri called out.

The world leaders returned to the gates; hints of impatience visible in their eyes. The world leader of the United States leaned forward on the bars.

"None of us find your evidence..." The world leader of the United States tapped his fingers against his arm before murmuring, "convincing."

"Convincing?" Uri scoffed. "What if the flesh is evidence of a new species of lizard?"

"We want you to look for evidence regarding the survivors, not animals."

World Leader Jordan stepped forward and looked up to the scorching sun hanging over Shamayim. "I'll admit it, Davida," Jordan ended harshly and lowered her head, "you are stuck in a rocky predicament where you need to really prove your worth."

Uri cocked her head as Jordan continued, "I could recommend some locations for you in order to cover more ground."

World Leader Jordan sent a document containing a second list of areas that had not been provided when Uri started her mission. Uri opened up the document and frowned when she saw that it was similar to the one for the town.

"Some of Shamayim's residents believe that someone still lives here," Jordan continued. "No one is certain about whom it could be, but some people claim to have seen someone working around this property—chopping wood, carrying in grocery bags—although no vehicle has been spotted. The Shamayim government has not received a distress call from this individual, but we plan to assist him or her."

Uri looked through the images of a mansion. It was advertised as a "House of the Future" despite the fact that the only futuristic quality was the shiny built-in appliances.

"Does the survivor have a name?" Uri asked. She looked up to see the world leader press her fingers together while she bit her lip in hesitation. Uri took the response as a "no" and asked another question.

"Are there any more occupants that have been seen? Family? Friends?"

World Leader Jordan grinned and responded with another sheepish "no."

Uri sighed and flipped through the images again.

There was no shadow that could be seen, nor any sign that the mansion was occupied. However, Uri could only go by the images provided. She looked in the corner of the images to see that they were taken a week before the Mysterious War. She could only imagine what the house would look like now after a year of neglect.

"It wouldn't be the Shadow, would it?" Uri asked.

World Leader Jordan cocked her head, and an irked grin stretched across her face. "The what?" she asked.

"One of the documents you gave me had an article about the town being tormented by something the towns-people called the Shadow."

Jordan squinted as she said, "I'm afraid I don't know what you are talking about, Sergeant."

Uri went back to looking through the images. "When I went to that town, I saw this shadow; it appeared to be human—the same one the townspeople described in the news article."

World Leader Jordan pressed her fingers together and lowered her eyelids.

"The Shadow might be a survivor," Uri said.

"Oh!" World Leader Jordan's eyes lit up, and she clapped her hands. "That changes everything!"

"How so?" Uri asked.

"What if the Shadow knows where the other survivors are?" World Leader Jordan proposed. "All you would need to do is catch up to them and gain enough of their trust so they will follow you to Shamayim."

"Gain their trust?" Uri asked.

Jordan frowned and gently rocked on her feet. "Well, we want survivors as soon as possible, so if you manage to gain this Shadow's trust, say, enough to let you approach them, then we'll have our survivors."

"I might need to promise the Shadow something in exchange," Uri said.

"Perfect!" World Leader Jordan exclaimed. "What do you plan to give them in exchange for their trust?"

A blank expression fell on Uri's face. She quickly realized that promising food and shelter wouldn't be enough for some survivors. She barely had anything that the survivors would most likely want or need.

"I have...information about Shamayim."

The world leaders looked at their monitors and then at each other.

"Well, Sergeant," World Leader Jordan said as she scratched her head, "that's a good start, but you'll need to think of something more...convincing."

"I have information about Shamayim that would be...appealing to the survivors," Uri added, "such as where to go for resources—"

"That is convincing!" Jordan cut Uri off. "Just letting the survivors know about this appealing information should help you to gain their trust. I have to go now. Good luck on finding those survivors!"

World Leader Jordan shut off her monitor and went back inside the office with the rest of the World Leaders, leaving Uri in silence.

CHAPTER 4

Uri wandered back to the Wastelands outside of her shelter to prepare for her next mission, searching for survivors. Her head shot up when she caught the sound of aluminum cans crashing together. She looked up and watched as a crow flew away from a trash pile causing some of the cans to shift.

She turned back as she caught the Shadow slip in and out of the corner of her eye. She turned again to see a strange maroon-colored substance leak from the spaces in the trash pile. The substance appeared to be moving the more she stared at it.

As Uri stepped closer to get a better look, another crow popped out of the trash pile and lunged for her eyes. Uri fell back as she watched a murder of crows fly upward from the spaces between the piles of garbage, cawing as they flew off in a black cloud. She tilted her head as the crows sped into the distance.

She pulled up the GPS on her communicator to locate the mansion that World Leader Jordan provided for her. "Uploading coordinates to the Gage Estate, your next destination for survivors," the GPS chimed. "Turn left!"

As Uri turned to the left and began walking, the GPS barked out impatiently, "No, turn right!"

Uri shrugged her shoulders and walked to the right. However, she received the same disapproving response that demanded that she turn to the left. The GPS kept up this strange list of directions, eventually guiding Uri into a zigzag pattern through the scrapyard.

"This is idiotic," Uri murmured.

"What was that?" the GPS growled furiously and pulled up its self-destruct sequence page.

"Nothing!" Uri barked at the GPS and allowed it to continue its strange directions to the estate. She shook the GPS a couple of times. It wasn't until she smacked it that it rebooted with a new set of instructions.

"Starting route to the Gage Estate on Six Westwood Street, go straight; you are on the fastest route and should arrive at two fifteen p.m."

"Amazing," Uri groaned, "the latest in crappy technology and I get to use it to find survivors."

Uri followed the coordinates, hoping the GPS was keeping her on the direct path, considering that she was only twenty feet away from her shelter.

"Keep going straight!" the GPS chimed. The GPS then rushed through a series of complex directions guiding Uri out of the scrapyard and into the desert. "Turn left, turn right, and go straight!"

Uri looked up to see that her GPS had directed her toward a highway. She took a deep breath as she bitterly clung to the patience she had left as she waited for the GPS's next direction. She looked to the monitor when she did not hear the GPS announce the next direction and saw that a reboot screen had appeared.

"Data corruption," the communicator announced. "Please restart your device and try again."

Uri completely shut off her communicator and stuffed it into her backpack before she continued down the highway, repeatedly murmuring "Westwood Street." Old, dusty cars were lined up along the freeway and continued down the off-ramps. She walked down the freeway listening to the sound of glass crunching beneath her feet.

Most cars were crushed together as a result of speeding. Some vehicles contained corpses. Their heads and shoulders were covered in the maroon slime, connecting their bodies to the dash and seats of their vehicles or to the outside of their cars. Some of the corpses had blood crusted over their ears as if they had been busted open. Uri peered into each of the vehicles at the red and black leeches squirming across the decomposing bodies.

Some corpses lay outside of their vehicles, some with broken bones and ripped clothing as if they had been in a fight. Blood crusted over purses, wallets, and older models of communicators.

She followed the road to an intersection. The lines of cars ended in a four-car collision in the middle of the intersection. The glass crackled beneath Uri's boots with each step she took. As she walked through the intersection, she murmured, "Westwood Street, where will I find Westwood Street if my GPS won't work?"

A green street sign snapped off of its hooks and landed face up on the asphalt in front of Uri. She looked down at the sign that read "Westwood Street."

"Well," she cocked her head and let out a faint laugh, "there's my sign."

She ran the rest of the way until she came to a forest that resembled the surrounding area where the survivors were located. Uri turned around in search of a mansion. She expected to see it in the distance, but the uneven ground and overgrowth buried the view ahead. Uri hiked through the overgrowth as it caved in beneath her feet with each step she took.

She saw a faint light toward the back of the forest and parted the draping plants. She stared at the sight as she walked into a rich, green meadow surrounded by the rest of the forest. Tree branches swayed with the calm breeze, revealing bright neon bluebirds constructing nests out of twigs and mud. Rabbits poked their heads out of their burrows and dove back in as Uri walked by.

A light-brown, lop-eared rabbit approached her. Uri reached down to pet the rabbit but pulled her hand back as its yellow fur shifted in the sunlight revealing a golden gloss. The rabbit then hopped away. Uri's eyes followed the rabbit as it hopped over to a six-legged fox that rested in the shade of the trees. The fox did not move or attack the rabbit as the rabbit snuggled between the fox's front legs.

She watched the fox gently lift its head in response to the rabbit and then lay it back down. Its eyelids twitched as the rabbit repositioned itself until it fell asleep against the fox's fur.

"That's strange," Uri said. She took a picture of the scene on her communicator before moving on to observe the rest of the animals. She lifted up her communicator to take a picture of a nest of uniquely colorful rabbits curled up against a tree. The rabbits lifted their heads and then dived down into a nearby burrow. Uri then looked up to see more of the neon bluebirds nesting in the tree over the rabbits' burrow. As she lifted up her communicator to take a picture, she saw the Shadow run in the background of her screen. She looked up from her communicator and saw the Shadow run toward a small hill that led to a trimmed archway in a hedge.

Uri chased after the Shadow. She was still unable to make out its features other than the blue veins visible against its pale skin whenever it ran in the sunlight. Uri watched the Shadow leave behind large drops of a slimy substance.

Uri stopped to examine the slime. It appeared similar to the maroon slime from the duffel bag she had found in the abandoned town.

She chased after the Shadow, making out more of its details. Maroon slime dripped down the uneven sleeves of the Shadow's sackcloth-like shirt and onto the ground, forming more leeches.

The Shadow sprinted away from Uri and jumped off a

nearby cliff. Uri skidded to a stop and looked down. The cliff was a mere five feet tall and led to a lower section of woods where the forest split into four paths. Uri looked up in response to the rustling and watched as the Shadow climbed onto the tree branches toward the fourth path on the right. Uri carefully slid down the side of the cliff and darted down the fourth path. Branches scraped against her uniform as she followed the Shadow through the rest of the forest.

Uri jumped down and ran on a narrow path lined with low intertwined trees. She crawled on the ground and looked behind her to see that the Shadow, now crouched beneath the trees, was crawling toward her. Uri squeezed out of the narrow opening and ran toward a small, four-foot untrimmed opening in a hedge. She exited through the opening that led her to another meadow.

Dead grass pierced the bottom of the hedge as weeds and stinging nettle reached up and grabbed at Uri's ankles. She looked at her communicator to see that this mansion was the same mansion that World Leader Jordan wanted her to investigate. Uri ran through the uncut grass and uneven ground toward the front door, trying not to trip. She reached out to ring the doorbell. She looked down to see that the bell was busted and the monitor above it was cracked from a small rock that lay on the ground beneath the bell.

Uri knocked on the door. "Hello, is anyone home?"

She listened for any noises alerting her that survivors lived there. Simple noises such as footsteps on the stairs or a dog barking would have comforted her. However, there were no noises.

Uri tried to look through the window and called out, "Hello? I've been sent by Shamayim to escort you to one of their locations!"

Once again, there was no response, only the gentle sounds of the breeze blowing through the trees and the noises of forest animals nervously responding to Uri's shouts.

"Do you know about Shamayim? I've been sent on a mission to take you there."

Uri listened for anyone to respond. Despite the mansion being on private property, the residents should have received some notification of the evacuation to Shamayim.

"They would have had to know," Uri whispered as she looked through the side windows for any signs of life. "Perhaps they left before I got here."

She pressed her ear against the door again, not a sound. She scrutinized the front porch for any decorative or high-tech key boxes, turning over each decoration on the porch while asking herself, "Would the owners leave a key to their house on their porch?"

She knocked on the door again to get whoever lived in the mansion to answer her, and the door creaked and fell off of its hinges, revealing a dark entryway. The heavy thumping of feet could be heard from upstairs.

"Sorry about the door!" Uri called out.

The entryway was lined with a large variety of carriers

and cages either empty or containing dead or dying animals. A pair of dead kiwis lay in a cramped cylinder bird cage, the corpse of a bloated young Doberman pinscher lay covered in flies in a large kennel, and the kennel next to it contained an agonized calico cat, scratching at its missing patches of fur and raw flesh.

Uri glanced at the other animals. All of them would be considered worthless to the world leaders as evidence of survivors.

She looked farther down the marble hallway and saw the Shadow standing at the end. It turned back to face Uri before gracefully dipping beneath the cobwebs that lined the hallway.

Uri chased after the Shadow. She watched as it slinked along the walls at the end of the hallway. It reached down and picked up something that appeared to be squirming in its hand and emitted what resembled a tiny scream. The Shadow then walked to another hallway. Uri followed at a distance as the screaming grew louder. The scream resembled the one from the leeches Uri found in the abandoned town.

She wandered down the hallway, screams continued in response to the tiles cracking beneath her boots. Some screams were short while others persisted. She looked into a room and found it filled with red and black leeches. Some of the leeches were gnawing on the bones of dead animals.

"How have you been alive this long?" Uri asked, staring at the leeches that covered the room. She looked down to see a hermit crab case containing one of the leeches. It pressed its mouth against the glass, the tiny mouths emitting a whisper. She picked up the case and ran back toward the hallway. She looked around the corner of the entrance to see the Shadow running back and forth across the hallway.

As the Shadow looked down the hallway, Uri ran back toward the entrance of the mansion. She ran out into the woods, looking back only to see the Shadow staring through the first floor's hallway window.

———————————⫸《◉》⫷———————————

Uri ran to the entrance of the scrapyard. She slowed to a brisk walk as she made her way back to her base to see if the Shadow had followed her.

Uri smiled at the leech while she felt for her door's handle. Her hand touched air, and she looked up to see that her door had been left wide open. Her short breaths changed to wheezing as she whispered, "I left the entrance of my base covered."

She clenched her teeth when she realized she did not have any weapons. Uri looked around the scrapyard for anything she could use as an improvised weapon.

She quietly stepped inside and jumped when she heard an ear-splitting voice say, "Hi! Are you here to look at the house?"

Uri backed up against the wall. The intruder's eyes

widened as he gently set his communicator on the ground and raised his hands above his head.

Uri's voice trembled with fear as she attempted to shout, "Wh-who are you? What are you doing inside my base?"

"Your base?" The intruder scratched his head with one hand and used the other hand to scroll through his monitor. He looked around the room in awe, completely oblivious to the fact that he was in a scrapyard and that Uri already claimed this area as her base.

"You do realize that everyone is gone"—Uri pointed to the wasteland outside her door—"right?"

"Everyone is gone?" The intruder laughed. "No one is ever too far away from Quick's Quick Real Estate Agency!" His eyes darted down to the leech that squirmed around its case.

"No pets!" he announced as he scribbled on his monitor.

Uri cocked her head and muttered, "Are you trying to be a smart-ass?"

Quick appeared to either ignore or not hear Uri's comment and continued his scrutiny of her base.

"Wait a minute!" Quick stopped to shove a brochure into Uri's face.

Uri hesitated and then accepted the brochure. She read the name of the agent and his slogan:

Kelvin Quick: For a Quick Closing.

A terrible pun used one too many times, Uri thought.

She lowered her backpack to the floor and pulled her communicator out of the top zipper. Quick swiped the communicator out of her hands, and she looked up to see him tuck it underneath his arm and smile.

"No time for games!" Quick said. "We need to settle the closing."

"Don't play stupid," Uri spat. "I need to relocate you!"

"Sorry, sweetheart"—Quick reached up to pinch Uri's cheek—"but I have a house to sell!"

Uri grabbed Quick by his shirt collar. "And I have a grenade and no reason for you to live."

Quick's eyes widened. He lifted his opened palms above his head. "Please," he stuttered, "I am not here to hurt you. I am here to help you."

Uri rolled her eyes at first but decided to see what Quick had to prove. "Like animals?" She looked up and down at the ripples in Quick's joints and stomach. "Other than for eating?"

"Er," Quick stuttered, "I used to volunteer at my community's animal shelter when I was in high school."

"Close enough." Uri pointed to the case containing the leech. "Bring that leech over here while I call my leaders."

Quick handed Uri's communicator back to her and he scurried to the entrance while Uri placed her call to Shamayim. When Quick returned, he set the cage containing the leech next to the monitor. A fuzzy voice was tuning in, and a black-and-white screen revealed a long line of people dancing and singing inaudible songs.

"This is Sergeant Uri, do you copy?" Uri shouted.

Unfortunately, no one could hear her over the booming

pop music and static. The screen shifted to color, and the music became slightly clear but still gave off a static noise. Uri continued waving and calling out until one of the dancers made eye contact and happily approached the monitor.

"Well, hi!" the responder shouted and leaned in to the camera where her poorly cut shirt revealed a rather terrifying amount of cleavage. Her entire body swayed. She was obviously too drunk to comprehend the situation and sloshed the liquid in the plastic cup in her hand onto the floor. Quick watched as the woman spoke without pressing the call button while a passerby slipped on the liquid she had spilled. She appeared to stop speaking and squinted, twisting strands of her long blond hair between her fingers. She then looked down at the control panel, laughed, and pushed the call button before slurring the words, "How can I help you?"

"I need the rescue team to take this survivor and leech back to Shamayim!" Uri shouted and pointed as Quick came into view of the camera.

"Oh yeahhh!" She laughed and turned to the crowd while shouting in a giggly voice, "Hey, rescue leader!"

Quick and Uri watched as a man in a silver suit and a plastic gold-colored fedora, all wrapped in toilet paper, came up to the monitor. "Hey!" he shouted in a peppy voice, "what's on TV?"

"I don't know!" The woman laughed and took another sip of her drink. "Let's see what else is on!"

"No wait!" Uri shouted as the call ended.

She held her head in her hand and growled. She flinched at a gentle tap on her shoulder and spun around to see Quick giving her a peculiar wave. She quickly masked her cold fear with a warm, joyful expression.

"We'll have you out shortly, Mr. Quick," she said pleasantly.

"Actually," Quick said, smiling, "if it helps any, I could try to call your world leaders on my communicator."

Uri reluctantly passed her communicator back to Quick and looked over his shoulder as he dispatched the call to the world leaders using his own communicator. After a single ring, a pleasant voice answered the call.

"Shamayim's main office, this is World Leader Jordan."

Uri pushed Quick closer to the screen as he put on his disturbing smile.

"Oh look, you found a survivor," Jordan said flatly. "We'll dispatch the search-and-rescue team immediately."

"Thank you." Uri grimaced as World Leader Jordan ended the call.

CHAPTER 5

Uri sat at the table in her base at about six the next morning, pressing a warm mug of coffee to her forehead while waiting for another mission from the world leaders.

"They had better accept that stupid leech and that idiotic survivor," Uri muttered as her eyes wandered down to look at the time on her communicator. She had been awake since three still thinking about the Shadow appearing in the abandoned town—how it seemed to be unharmed by the prism lizard, how it didn't go to her for help, and how it didn't attack her but remained in the distance as if it wanted her to follow it.

"Is that the same Shadow?" Uri asked herself. "How is it able to keep up with me? Does it always know where I am? Is it one of the survivors, and are they simply afraid of others, which is why they are afraid of me? Or do they not want to be rescued?"

She wondered if the Shadow was linked to the prism lizard because it appeared to have been hidden behind the wreckage in which the prism lizard died.

Uri heard her communicator chime, and she snatched it up.

Sergeant Uri,

The evidence of the leech is in for testing right now.

Your next mission: There's a family theme park, Timmy's Town, that's located right behind your base. We need you there now to locate survivors.

The World Leaders

Timmy's Town? Uri scratched her head as she opened the archives for the theme park provided on her communicator. She only received bits and pieces of information, such as claims from locals when the park was over a century old or that the costumes were actually robots that would turn on and off whenever they wanted to, simply a collision of criticisms.

She looked up in response to a scratching noise. A rusted can tumbled down from a hole in the ceiling and landed in a pile of garbage by the entrance. Rats scattered from the corners of the base and squeezed through the cracks in the walls.

She pulled the cloth down and exited her base backward to see what the world leaders meant. She stared at the pile of garbage until her eyes caught the point of a prop mountain. Uri ran around to see the rusting entrance of the theme park the world leaders had described in her next mission, trying to make out the mix of old colors and parts.

The dilapidated theme park's faded paint chipped away with the wind as it provided an eerie symphony of creaks

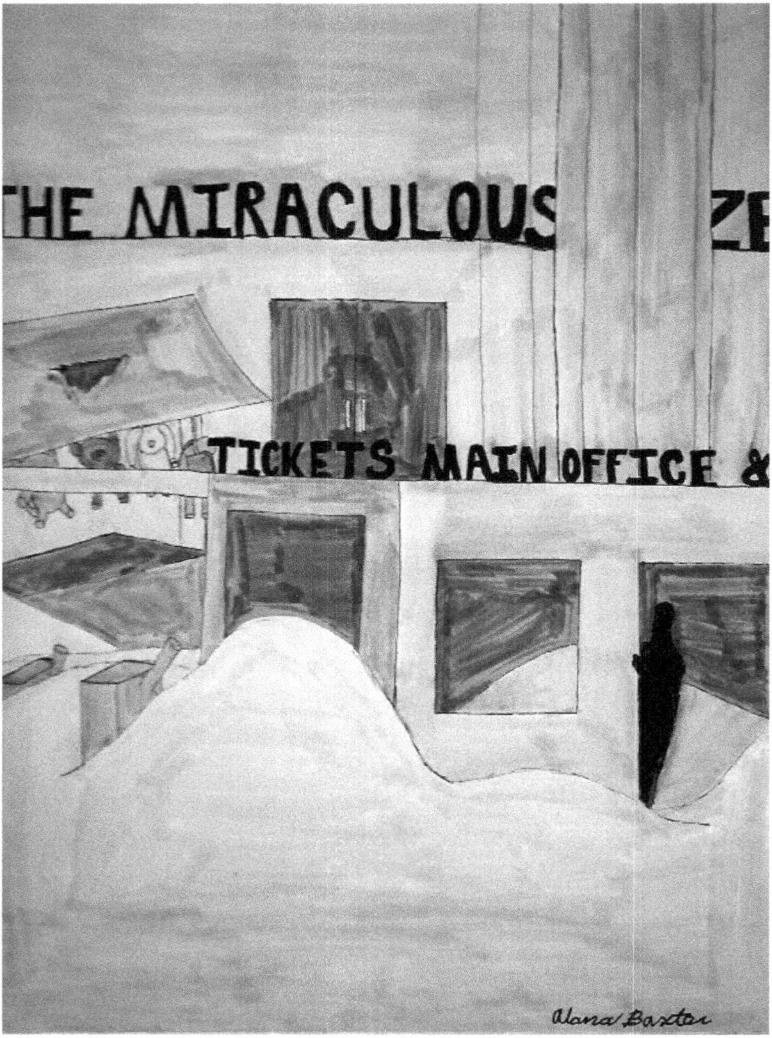
THE MIRACULOUS
TICKETS MAIN OFFICE &
Alana Baxter

and groans when it blew through the steel attractions.

"How?" Uri asked herself, "how have I never noticed an entire theme park directly behind my base?"

The wind swept up the sand and carried it through the entrance of the park, directing Uri's attention to the center of the main entrance where a ticket booth, restrooms, and a building labeled "Main Office and Lost Children's Center" were set up. The door was propped open by its doorstop, collecting the sand and litter from the scrapyard.

Uri watched the Shadow poke its head out of the entrance. It waved its hand as if it were beckoning Uri to follow it. The Shadow then ducked back inside the office.

Uri waited before following at a distance. She looked at the spotty rays of sun lighting a path along a rubber cream-colored floor. Sand and litter swayed with the breeze, flowing through the entrance. Uri looked down the office's hall and saw the Shadow take a sharp turn to the right. She watched as it then ran to the left side of the hallway. Uri crept forward in response to the Shadow's movement. When she reached the edge of the hall, she peered around the corner to see another hallway with a row of doors on both sides. A warm breeze flowed from an open door at the end of the hall.

"I have no weapons, I have food and water, but who knows if that will be enough to coax this survivor out of hiding," Uri told herself.

She slowly approached the end of the hall. As she got closer, a buzzing noise similar to a swarm of insects sounded from the room the Shadow had entered. The buzzing then changed to what sounded like a crowd of people whispering.

"Survivors?" Uri wondered as she approached the room where the door lay inside. On the floor she saw a plaque near the fallen door that read "Lost Children's Center." Uri then noticed that the door handle was coated in the maroon slime. She pushed on the wood of the door, and the slime trailed off. Her eyes followed the trail of slime along the whitewashed walls.

The crowd of voices grew louder again and then subsided. Then silence.

Uri crept into the room and felt her boot slip. She looked down to see more of the slime, creating another trail along the floor and up the wall. Uri collected the slime in a plastic bag and looked around the rest of the room.

"Could an animal have done this?" Uri asked. She examined the slime a little longer. "Then again, what kind?"

The slime led to a door on the other side of the Lost Children's Center. Uri exited the door and stepped into the park, her hand still gripping the door.

She watched the Shadow run across the amusement park. It almost appeared to be dancing as it moved.

After the Shadow was out of Uri's sight, she heard a whispering sound in the park's atmosphere. Uri rubbed her forehead and grunted. She stumbled back inside the Lost Children's Center and knelt to the ground.

"God," Uri gasped, "why are those whispers so loud?"

The whispers grew louder and spread into the hallway

to the outside of the office. Uri tried to find the source of the voices as she laid her face on the ground, covered the back of her head with her hands, and listened to a squishing noise beneath her boots. A liquid formed around Uri's knees, clinging to her pant legs.

The whispers ceased, and Uri pulled her hands away from her head and looked up. She looked around the room to see that the walls, ceiling, floor, and furniture were now completely coated in thick layers of maroon slime.

"You're new," said a voice belonging to a small child.

Uri listened for the voice again but remained crouched on the floor of the Lost Children's Center. She stretched her hand out and picked up the maroon slime. She watched in awe as the slime molded around the spaces between her fingers.

"Is the slime a living thing?" Uri wondered.

The slime ran off of her fingers and connected back with the slime on the floor. Uri rolled up the leftover slime, forming a ball between her thumb and index finger. She became hypnotized by the slime as a collection of whispers filled the room, growing more audible.

"We are very much alive," one of the whispers said.

Uri jumped when the slime squirmed into the palm of her hand and rolled out into a wormlike shape. The worm molded itself until it looked more like an undernourished leech. Its mouth opened revealing thousands of tiny mouths behind a row of razor-sharp teeth.

Silence fell over the room again, and Uri dropped the

leech. The leech shifted, and its red and black gradient skin glimmered in the spots of sunlight. It emitted a noise resembling a shriek and reverted to whispering.

The slime on the walls made a subtle shift, and the buzzing noise continued. The buzzing traveled throughout the park, and the sounds across the park became audible. The drips from distant grease spills in a burnt restaurant resembled gunshots. The breeze caused fingernail-like squeaks in the tilted, rusted Ferris wheel. The creak of the roller coaster's tracks produced a ghastly wail.

Uri stood up rapidly, watching the slime break off of her pant legs.

"Come outside, please," the voice said.

Uri watched as the slime pulled away from the door that led to the theme park. She turned back and noticed that the entrance to the Lost Children's Center at the other end of the room was still untouched by the slime. Uri ran toward the entrance, and the slime molded over the door, seeping through the tiny spaces between the door and the wall.

"Please stay," the voice squeaked. "I promise I won't hurt you."

"Tell me who you are first!" Uri shouted.

"I am a..." Static replaced the voice, and Uri covered her ears in response to the noise. "But I trust you," the voice said in its childlike tone. "Now look around you."

Uri followed the voice's request. The room became jet black. A glowing white silhouette of the door on the side of the room appeared where there was once a window.

"Please walk through that door," the voice said.

"You have to tell me who you are first," Uri said. She looked around frantically for the real source of the voice. Then she tried to find the leech that formed from the slime in her hands, but the slime continued to shift like water in the ocean.

"We're here to demonstrate what happened to your Earth," a collection of voices said. "We exist to help humans like you understand the new Earth you live in now."

"What do you mean?" Uri asked.

The collection of voices snickered. "You'll see soon enough. There should be a path forming in front of you; please follow it."

"I don't trust you," Uri said.

"You'll trust us eventually," the voices replied, sounding more patient than before. "Please follow the path in front of you."

Uri shivered as she looked around for a path. She looked down and watched as the slime split, revealing a glowing white walkway in front of her. The path led to a glowing white archway where the window overlooking the park had been originally.

"The Shadow was out there," Uri said.

"We will protect you from the Shadow," the voices said.

"How?" Uri asked sarcastically. "Will you make me invisible?"

"No," the voices said flatly. "We will guide you toward areas where the Shadow will never find you," the voices hummed, "that is, if you will trust us."

Uri looked back at the archway. "Wasn't there a window there?" she asked.

"Yes," the voices sighed, "but it is not there now. Remember, you can trust us."

Uri looked toward the section of the room where the entrance had been but saw that it was replaced by a wall of maroon slime. She gasped when she realized that she could see the hallway through the wall. A glowing human silhouette Uri recognized as the Shadow was running down the hallway and toward the Lost Children's Room.

The Shadow jumped against the door causing the wall of slime to shake.

"That wall won't last," the voices hissed. "Run!"

Uri sprinted through the archway and outside into the main park. She watched as the Ferris wheel and carousel started moving without lights or noises.

"Your leaders lied to you," the voices said. "There are no survivors here."

"Who are you?" Uri asked again, growing agitated from not receiving an answer.

"We've already told you," the voices said.

"All I heard was static," Uri replied.

The voices chuckled. "You'll be able to understand us eventually; now, if you would be so kind as to let us accompany you in your search for survivors."

As the rides and attractions slowed to a halt, Uri heard a loud caw. She looked up to see a crow from the scrapyard dive for her head. Uri dropped to the ground, feeling the wind from the crow's wings rush across her body as it passed over her. Another one of the leeches fell from the crow's feathers, landing on the ground in front of Uri. Thousands of leeches crawled out from beneath the theme park's structures and squirmed toward her.

Uri stood up and ran into a building with a sign that read "The Miraculous Maze" and stood still as the door behind her slammed shut.

CHAPTER 6

U ri listened for the voices again but remained still on the floor of the Miraculous Maze. She extended her hand out and picked up the maroon slime and watched in awe as the slime molded around the spaces between her fingers.

The room brightened to a scarlet red as the leeches squirmed into the holes along the walls. They wailed, "Sergeant Uri!" Their voices echoed down the first hall of the maze, beckoning Uri to follow. As Uri wandered through the maze, the leeches spoke.

"We want to grant you the opportunity to locate survivors with ease by taking you to areas where no human would think to look, areas where you will find others to help you and areas where you can navigate easily without a GPS unit."

Uri stopped and squinted. "What's the catch?"

"No catch," the leeches said cheerfully. "We're here to help you!"

"You've already said that," Uri responded. She rubbed her temples as the whispering continued. "Yet somehow I still don't believe you."

The whispering increased to an earsplitting scream and then decreased back to a soft whisper. Uri covered her ears as the overwhelming sounds traveled throughout the maze.

She felt her foot hit a stack of empty cardboard boxes, knocking them to the ground. As the last of the boxes tumbled to the floor, the room grew quiet. Uri looked around frantically when she heard the leeches sing, "That's not good!"

"You sounded oddly cheerful for a second," Uri said. She glanced over her shoulder, waiting to see if the Shadow was closing in on her. Her eyes confused the leeches' movements for the Shadow. "I'm starting to wonder if you're working for the Shadow."

As Uri said this, she felt her foot miss a step, and she fell a short way into a ball pit at the bottom of the maze.

"Ouch!" the leeches shouted. "Revenge does not feel good, does it?"

Uri scrambled to her feet and continued trudging through the ball pit. She brushed off the leeches' comments and asked, "So, leeches, care to tell me what you know about the Shadow? Or the Mysterious War for that matter?"

"Well..." the leeches said.

Uri picked up on their hesitant whispers before they finished with a brief "no" and let out a series of loud laughs.

Uri scoffed and climbed onto a plastic ramp where she was able to see more of her immediate surroundings. She looked back to see the Shadow standing at the entrance of the ball pit, outlined by the small amount of sunlight that leaked in. She tried to walk fast but slipped down the rest of the ramp. Plastic balls gathered over her. She brought herself up to her knees and watched as a trail of maroon slime dripped down the ramp, making it slippery. Uri picked herself up and pushed her way through the plastic balls to the exit. She listened as the plastic balls clinked together behind her. She looked back again and saw that the Shadow had hopped down into the ball pit as well and was now pursuing her.

Uri forgot about the slime and the leeches as she ran through the rest of the pit to the emergency exit in the corner of the room. She flung the door open and ran down a hallway, refusing to see if the Shadow was still behind her. As she ran, she heard more of the leeches' cries to not leave them behind. Uri ran down a long spiral staircase, her boots clinking against the metal with each step she took. As she moved closer to the ground, she let out a sigh of relief as a large double door, similar to one found in a hospital, came into view.

"Finally," Uri gasped, "the exit."

She rushed to the door. Each side had a window panel where she could see the next attraction of the theme park. She pushed open the door and sprinted into the center of the park. Then she looked back at the door to watch it slam shut.

"No evidence of survivors," Uri sighed, "but I'm out."

She reached up to wipe the sweat from her forehead

and quickly pulled her hand away. Drops of the maroon slime trickled down her hand leaving purple stains.

"What is that from?" Uri asked as she examined the stain.

"Why are you worried about the slime?" the leeches said. "You should be worried that the Shadow is still chasing you."

Uri turned around to see the Shadow burst through the emergency exit of the maze. She continued running until she heard a nearby wailing and saw a group of leeches crawling along the ground toward her. One of the leeches clung tightly to a piece of broken glass. It let out a small cry as the glass pierced through it, oozing maroon slime. It reminded Uri of the prism lizard and how it rolled about the town attempting to inflict itself with as much pain as possible.

Uri's eyes widened at the sound of structures collapsing. She looked up as the roller coaster folded into the Ferris wheel, creating a twisted flower of titanium as it landed onto the carousel. Tracks from the roller coaster fell onto the ticket booth and continued to crush the scrapyard.

Uri looked over to where the roller coaster's tracks fell. Beneath them was a compressed pile of various pieces of cloth and steel.

"Of course, it crushed my base," Uri sighed. As she turned away from the wreckage, her communicator chimed. She looked down to see a message from World Leader Jordan regarding her next mission.

Sergeant Uri,

We've lost sight of the theme park. Your next mission: There is a strange building located in the center of a forest about fifteen miles from your base. We need you there now.

World Leader Lior Jordan

As Uri pulled up the directions for the next area, she felt someone standing behind her. She turned to see a faint movement from behind a pile of old garbage bags. More red and black leeches inched their way out of the spaces between the plastic trash bags. Uri felt the world around her close in as the leeches' whispers grew louder.

She massaged her temples in pain as she fought her way away from the scrapyard in order to escape the leeches.

CHAPTER 7

U ri uploaded the coordinates for her next mission. She realized that locating survivors in a "strange building" would be the easiest part; trying to herd them to Shamayim would be another story. She could only show the survivors pictures and videos that depicted daily life on Shamayim through their easy access to fresh food and shelter, as well as any other necessities that Shamayim's government predicted the survivors would want.

"That will not necessarily make the survivors want to go," Uri said as she hiked up a mound of sand that appeared on her communicator. She tried to figure out where she was, other than the middle of the desert.

Uri took into deep consideration that between the short time of the Mysterious War and now, an infinite number of events would have taken place to alter the personalities and attitudes of what were possibly once respectful and kind individuals.

These supposed survivors, who suffered through the loneliness of a barren world after a war robbed them of their happiness, dignity, and hope, would be so engulfed in their new lifestyle that they would either see Uri as an ally, a threat, or a meal depending on each individual's situation.

"Then again," Uri hesitated, "the survivors might be happy to see help arrive, that is, if the Mysterious War didn't leave them with any type of trauma that would make them change their minds."

Uri held her hands against the back of her head. She could still hear the chattering from the leeches as she walked through the thick piles of sand.

"Why leeches?" Uri asked herself. "How are they able to speak? What are they capable of doing other than destroying rats' ear canals or whispering useless directions to the people who trespass on their territory?"

She thought about how the leeches appeared to have no interest in mindlessly attacking her. Instead, they seemed to want some type of power. "I'm assuming power over my whole being," Uri said. She looked back at her communicator. A large section of green took up half of the screen as she moved forward. Uri saw a thick area of forest ahead of her. She looked back and saw that the remains of the theme park in the desert slowly grew tinier as she moved forward.

After walking another ten miles away from the scrapyard, Uri looked up at the tips of trees in the distance. "How can I go from a barren desert to a rainforest in twenty miles?"

She pushed through the trees, peering into the spaces between the plants to see teal and black widow spiders the size of house cats crawling up and down the tree trunks.

More monstrous insects emitted clicking noises while

birds mimicked them. Uri watched as a tiny, bright yellow frog inched its sticky webbed feet up a tree. A neon bluebird dived down, snatched the frog in its beak, and ducked back into the tree's leaves. Uri pulled the branches apart to get a closer look at the bird and immediately pulled her hands out of the tree branches. The bird was caught in one of the spider webs; it squirmed and let out loud tweets indicating its peril. The frog slipped out of the bird's beak and was trapped in the web as well.

Uri waited and watched as one of the teal spiders crawled down its web. It vomited a blue fluid over the bird's body before proceeding to devour it, as well as the frog. Uri took a picture of the spider, as well as one of a living neon bluebird and one of a living bright yellow frog.

"Then again," Uri told herself, "that mansion was shrouded by a dense rain forest, and it took a notification from the world leaders for me to find it; same for the amusement park."

As she walked through the woods, she carefully observed the colorful collection of animals that dominated this area. Blood-red beetles the size of an adult human's hand crawled up the sides of overgrown trees. Bright blue birds with feathers that opened up like cloth fans on top of their heads unleashed earsplitting caws as they circled the forest in search of sustenance. Tiny adaptations of the prism lizard scurried up and down the sides of the trees, emitting low hissing noises as they dived away from the birds' attacks.

"These creatures don't really appear to belong here,"

Uri said to herself. "They're too exotic."

As she moved deeper into the woods, Uri looked around at the variety of creatures. Some of the birds let out warning squawks to other members of their species and flew from their branches as Uri passed under them.

"But how did they get here?" Uri wondered.

She watched as more of the red and black leeches crawled out of the shadows and overgrowth. She covered her ears as she attempted to drown out their chaotic whispers and focus on her mission.

The sun poked through the branches, brightening the open spaces in the forest. Multiple pairs of eyes became visible in the shadows, blinking intermittently. Loud chirping noises emitted from the foliage as the animals reacted to the light.

Uri looked down at the trail to avoid stepping on and angering any types of animals that might want to attack her. "The only thing I don't want to run into is that Shadow," she said. "What does it even want from me? He or she or whatever it wishes to be called appeared to not need any help."

She brushed more of the tree branches out of her face and caught glimpses of various unusual eyes from the forest creatures. Their eyes appeared to glow. She flinched when she caught a set of dark brown human eyes staring directly at her from the shadows.

Uri tilted her head to her right, and the eyes followed her movement. She stepped to her left, and the eyes bounced along the shadows until they were in front of her again. Uri

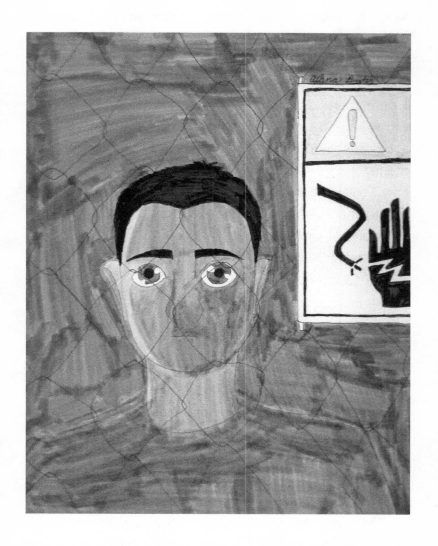

leaned closer to the eyes. She caught a low buzzing noise; however, it did not appear to resemble one of the insects. As Uri leaned closer to the eyes, a firm yet youthful voice broke the silence.

"Stop! The fence is electric."

Uri looked down at the eyes and saw a young face form around them as the speaker stepped into the light. This person appeared to be a teenager. Uri guessed he would be about seventeen years old. Midnight-black hair reflected the patch of sunlight. His clothes consisted of a simple dark gray T-shirt, black sports pants, and black sports shoes.

Uri immediately thought about the survivors. "Are you a survivor?" Uri asked.

"Survivor?" The boy cocked his head.

Uri scratched her head nervously. *Why would I ask a teenager about survivors?*

"I... don't understand," the boy said. "Why are you here? The academy is supposed to be hidden from all eyes."

Uri's head jolted to where the boy was looking, and she saw eight identical dark gray skyscrapers joined together by a one-story, rectangular titanium building. Children ranging from five to eighteen years of age ran and walked in and out of the mist that drifted from the rain forest. Uri tried to get a better look at the academy's atmosphere.

"This is a school?" she asked.

The boy's shoulders became tense, and he placed his hands over his mouth. Uri squinted; tiny silhouettes took the shapes of children playfully chasing each other across a patch of damp asphalt. The boy looked back when one of the taller children shouted, "Hey, Héctor! Who is that?"

Uri looked into the distance. Taller silhouettes were the shape of adults in their early twenties to early fifties patrolling the sector. One of the high school students briefly looked to Uri's direction, tapped the shoulder of another student next to him, and pointed to Uri.

"Why are you here?" the high school student shouted. "Are you lost?"

"But seriously," the boy at the fence asked, "why are you here? Why are you dressed like a soldier?"

Uri considered how she would respond. She knew that some survivors would be slow to trust her. "I'm searching for survivors," she said. "They're a group of people who were registered to live in a city called Shamayim, which is where I live."

She caught the boy's glare and took a couple of steps back, ready to retreat to a safe location where she could contact Shamayim. The boy's glare turned into a look of curiosity as he hesitantly responded, "So you're on...a search-and-rescue team?"

"That's correct," Uri said. "When I asked if you were a survivor..." She began but became distracted by one of the adults who had stopped patrolling the asphalt and gave her an icy glare. Uri realized that she needed to quickly wrap up her search-and-rescue mission. "I wanted to learn more about the academy. I've heard a lot about it."

That wasn't the right thing to say, she said to herself.

The boy narrowed his eyes. "How did information about the academy leak out?"

Uri thought, *Great, now what do I say?*

She realized that even walking by a barbed-wire perimeter fence would arouse suspicion. Uri nervously twitched and watched as the adult who had made eye contact earlier approached the fence. She needed to get these survivors to go to Shamayim.

She shrunk as the older man growled, "Who are you and how did you find us?"

"I'm..." Uri paused.

She realized she'd made herself appear even more suspicious. She looked back at the older man and noticed that he had turned on the communicator in his hand, ready to announce Uri's intrusion. Realizing she could be in trouble, she quickly conjured up a lie.

"I'm here for a job interview," Uri said.

A sly smile stretched across the older man's face. "Is that so?" he asked. "I take it you've already spoken with the principal and vice principal?"

"Yes," Uri said.

"You must be thrilled to see them after...where are you from?" the older man asked.

Uri looked around the school for any hints regarding the name of the principal and vice principal. "I'm from an allying city," Uri lied.

She wondered if the school would even want to listen to her. She also considered how she would escape in the event that these people decided to attack her instead of listen to her. She even wondered if she would be able to strike a deal with this school in hopes of bringing students to Shamayim.

"You'll have to speak to the heads of the academy." The older man nodded toward the entrance of the building and turned back to Uri with an evil expression across his face.

———— ◦《◉》◦ ————

The guards on the roof of the academy's main entrance signaled each other through the long process of opening the gate. The iron gates slid open to reveal six more guards on the ground, waiting to direct Uri to the front desk. Out of the corner of her eye, Uri caught at least two more guards on the ground, four more guards in the shadows of the buildings, and two more at the entrance of the main office building, which was where Uri was being forcefully guided.

She glanced over to where a handful of the lower-grade students were bunched together by another gate. That gate separated the main entrance of the academy from the black-top toward the back of the grounds where she met the student and the older man. The lower-grade students made negative remarks upon seeing Uri, while the upper-grade students gently hushed them and tried to direct them away from the gate. Uri tried to get a glance of the boy she met. The students continued to build up toward the front and crowded out the rest of the students as she was guided inside.

Uri looked around the hallways. Lower-grade students quickly looked up at her from their bedrooms and then focused back on their assignments, while the upper-grade students either blocked those entrances with their bodies or slammed and locked their doors.

High school students conversed with each other in whispers that remained audible. "Isn't she a little old to be a student?" "She looks too sane to be an instructor." "You're in the wrong place, bitch." "Hey, baby, are you lost?"

The students shouted more remarks. Some of the older students slammed their fists against the entryways as Uri passed by their rooms. She rolled her eyes and continued down the long and winding hallways.

"I dealt with the same vague threats when I first joined the LIES program," She told herself as an emotionless expression fell over her face.

She heard some of the students laughing, and she looked up at a door with "F-3" crudely etched into the wood.

The room was set up like a meeting room with old furniture, including a wooden table and mismatched chairs that ranged from bar stools to office chairs with pieces of fabric ripped away by either an animal or a human.

Uri walked by the bookshelves that covered the wall spaces. She scanned the titles hoping to find anything regarding the Hawkinses, the Shadow, or even Shamayim.

Did this academy receive any notice for Shamayim? Uri thought.

As she tilted one book back, she heard a voice.

"What are you doing?"

Uri jolted and turned around to see the other man she had met at the gate.

"I was only looking," Uri said as she quickly took her position at the meeting table and waited for an opportunity to interject Shamayim into the interview.

The man placed a stack of applications in front of Uri. "Let's cut to the chase," he said. "I'm Instructor Jaime Márquez. I serve as the heads of the academy's representative, and I will place you in a career of the academy's choosing based on your talents."

Uri glanced over the first page and leaned forward in her seat. "Actually, I'm not here for a job interview, Mr. Márquez. I'm here on a rescue mission."

"Keep trying to talk your way out of this," Márquez said and rolled his eyes. "I've heard it all."

Uri tapped her fingers against the table. "I'm part of a military organization called LIES. I'm here to rescue a group of people known as 'survivors' and return them to a city called Shamayim, which is how I happened across your academy."

Márquez stared and squinted at Uri.

Uri tapped her fingers against the table. "Are you familiar with the city known as Shamayim?"

Márquez responded with a firm "no," and a look of suspicion formed on his face.

"Shamayim is where I come from; it is one of many refugee cities around the world," Uri said, stretching her arms out. "I've been sent into the Wastelands, which is the land outside of one of the many refugee cities around the world constructed to maintain and protect the survivors."

Márquez scratched his head and murmured, "I've heard stranger stories."

"Once you're in Shamayim, you should be able to start a new academy." Uri thought about her words for a minute. "But you probably wouldn't be as well received as you are here."

Márquez cocked his head. "Not well received?" He sneered. "How come?"

"The refugee cities prefer more civilized inhabitants," Uri said. "They uphold strict laws in order to aid the citizens in maintaining a more comfortable lifestyle."

Uri watched as Márquez raised his eyebrows.

"Yet you still come to us to offer your services," Márquez hissed. "That's one civilized city."

"You see…" Uri took out her communicator and pulled up the blueprints for Shamayim. "Shamayim is one of the many cities that was constructed to bring the nations of the world together. In other words, it was meant as a way to achieve world peace. However, moving civilians in was rushed due to the Mysterious War."

"The what?" Márquez asked.

"The Mysterious War, in which people around the world kept slowly fighting each other, eventually coining the phrase 'Mysterious War,'" Uri said.

"Sounds like either a virus or everyone was slowly losing

their ability to tolerate one another," Márquez said. "What did your LIES program do about it?"

"The military is incredibly passive," Uri said. "They stay back and simply guard these refugee cities."

"A passive military?" Márquez cringed. "Then why are you here? I would think that you would want to live in a comfortable setting as opposed to the Wastelands, as you call our territory."

"I get that it sounds unbelievable," Uri said as she opened the advertisements for Shamayim on her communicator to show Márquez. "I was the only one who volunteered to search for survivors."

"Why would your military only depend on volunteers?" Márquez asked. "There should be a law when it comes to rescuing people."

"Unfortunately, there isn't," Uri said. "Sadly, luxury won over aiding others, but right now I plan to get into contact with my commanders, and we'll work together to save the academy."

"Commanders?" Márquez snorted. "You said you were a sergeant."

"Yeah," Uri sneered, "that's what they want me to believe."

CHAPTER 8

U ri placed a call to Shamayim's LIES wing. She looked around the room again, still hoping that she wouldn't be attacked. Her computer made a sharp ring with a notification that her call went directly to voice mail. Uri broke out in a cold sweat as she reentered Shamayim's number and looked up to see that Márquez remained seated, reviewing a clipboard of notes. Uri turned back to her communicator when a sharp chime alerted her that her call went directly to voice mail, again. She nervously rapped her fingers against the table as another call after another went to voice mail.

"My leaders must be attending an important meeting," she said and faintly laughed.

Márquez hummed in thought. "You get one more chance," he sneered.

Uri resorted to calling one of the governor's personal communicators, and the screen indicated that it was being answered. A grotesque scene appeared before Márquez and Uri. All of the world leaders crowded in and out of their monitor's camera. Uri noticed someone lift a bright red cocktail off of the computer desk as she swung around near the monitor, chatting with a soldier. Then she lifted her glass and shouted as if to toast before bringing it back to her lips, causing drops to fall onto their computer's controls. World Leader Gray could be seen in the background surrounded by five to six party attendants. He threw his hands into the air and created a series of gestures both obscene and polite, and the attendants collectively laughed. Another party attendant jumped up onto the meeting room table, turning around with a half-empty beer bottle in her hand. The party attendant on the ground next to her reached for the hem of her skirt and started rolling it up. Uri quickly shut off her monitor before she could see anymore, her face red with shame.

She then felt a hand wrap tightly around her neck, and she felt the table shake as Márquez brought his other hand down on it in a fist.

"You call that an important meeting?" Márquez growled. "What kind of jackasses do you take us for?"

Drops of sweat trickled down Uri's temples. She dispatched a call to a different branch of Shamayim's government, and Márquez returned to his seat. Once again, the call was answered, only this time there was no one at the keypad to communicate. The clink of a glass could be heard, and Uri's eyes dropped to the bottom of the screen to see that a margarita glass had been knocked onto the keypad. Its yellow-green contents trickled down into the grooves of the machinery, inching its way into the computer's wiring and causing the screen to shut off.

Uri watched in horror as the monitor faded to black, paired with the noise from the empty static.

She resorted to making a direct call to a branch agency that she hoped would at least hear her out. "Pick up, pick up, pick up…" Uri clinched her hand into a fist and pressed it into the wood of the table. To her surprise, she was immediately connected to the main LIES office.

"Hello, LIES Corporation," a man sighed, almost yawning, as he answered the call without making eye contact.

Uri's eyes widened at the littered site. She could feel Márquez's glare as she watched one of the employees at the desk set a plate of some unrecognizable meal on top of a stack of documents labeled "Important!"

"Sergeant Uri! Sergeant Davida Uri of the LIES World Marine Corps!" Uri announced in a firm tone, attempting not to run over her words, "I have successfully located sur—"

"Hold on," the receiver interrupted. He typed three words on his keyboard and paused to read whatever he had typed before typing a four-letter word. His sluggish typing caused Uri to sink into her chair.

"Could you please hurry up? This is urgent," Uri told the receiver. "I am about to be killed."

"Rude," the receiver scoffed. His image went out, and the automatic voice on Uri's computer read in an upbeat voice, "Call ended!"

"No," Uri gasped as Márquez slammed the palms of his hands against the table and shouted, "What the hell was that?"

Uri nervously tapped her fingers on the desk. "Let me try a different number."

Márquez hesitated and sat back in his chair. Uri scrolled through her contacts and landed on "World Leader Himura." She pushed the contact button and waited nervously for World Leader Himura to answer. She forgot to check if she would be on a break at the hour or in a meeting.

Uri took a deep breath when she saw that Márquez's chair was empty. She looked over her shoulder to see that he was leaning over her, his hands tightly gripping the top of her chair.

She ended the call and dialed the number to LIES's main office. She simply listened to the voice on her communicator repeat, "Calling LIES branch," as her heart raced. Uri twitched. The final ring on her communicator chimed, and her eyes focused back onto the video.

"World Leader...Oh." World Leader Himura ceased her greeting as she assessed the scenario. Márquez's head shot up toward the communicator.

"M-ma'am," Uri responded in a shaky voice, "I found those survivors."

———⊰⦿⊱———

A LIES armored vehicle recklessly sped through the forest. Uri watched through the spaces between her fingers as the vehicle pushed over a weak tree, killing the inhabitants of the tree, and stopped mere inches from the electric fence. She saw Principal Smith and Vice Principal Davis run up beside her. She looked to her sides to see that both of them watched with irritation and, with angry expressions, turned to Uri.

"Great," Principal Smith hissed. "There goes a section of our cover!"

"What is going on?" Vice Principal Davis sneered. His cold eyes pierced Uri's mind as he ranted. "Your leaders could have parked outside of the forest. We would have sent someone out to guide them to the academy's main office!"

Uri held her hand against her forehead and took deep breaths while she attempted to contact the crew to give better instructions. She only managed to get as far as the recorder's communication monitor, and then text appeared across her screen requesting a voice recording. She looked back at the vehicle and watched as World Leader Jordan stumbled onto the uneven ground, planting her feet firmly before almost falling into a nearby swamp.

Uri stared in disappointment as World Leader Jordan meandered up to the group, clearing her throat in the midst of stuttering her sentence.

"Oh my God." She took several deep breaths before she could speak again. She approached Uri first, leaning into her face while speaking. "Excuse me, Sergeant Uri, you have done well."

Uri was distracted by the scent of alcohol on her breath. She swayed as she walked and attempted to balance herself, clearly drunk and unaware of her surroundings. Uri felt the burning glares of Márquez and the academy principals as the other world leaders stepped out from their vehicles.

The students and guards lined up behind the fence as World Leader Jordan approached Principal Smith and Vice Principal Davis.

"Why did you destroy our forest?" Principal Smith shouted as she pointed toward the academy. "You couldn't have parked somewhere else?"

"Ma'am," World Leader Jordan said, "I'm terribly sorry. We did not know where to park."

Principal Smith turned to Uri and frowned.

Somone in a LIES military uniform stepped out of one of the vehicles with a wooden crate and placed it in front of World Leader Jordan. Jordan then motioned to another soldier to stand up on the crate with a megaphone.

Uri looked to Márquez. She caught a glimpse of the first teenager she had met waving to her from behind the fence. She ran over to the fence, and he introduced himself.

"Chávez," the teenager said, "Héctor Chávez. Anyway, what are they doing?" He motioned to World Leader Jordan.

"They are trying to make Shamayim sound appealing," Uri said. "Basically, they're a bunch of talking heads who have no ambitions in life so they burn up their energy on lavish parties and making themselves sound as heroic as possible, since they don't need to do much on Shamayim."

Uri rubbed her forehead. "Their jobs are to just run everything."

"Into what," Chávez cringed, "the ground?"

"Basically," Uri replied. Then she continued to listen to World Leader Jordan's speech.

"Here's the deal, kids!" Jordan pointed toward the forest as she shouted through a megaphone, "We have everything you need: food, education, and leisurely activities for everyone. We are willing to let you leave this dead land for a better life! You will not need to worry about self-defense, careers, or colleges anymore. We will provide!"

Some of the students whispered questions to each other, some nodded, and others shook their heads and whispered, "This is ridiculous."

The students then looked to Principal Smith and Vice Principal Davis, all with the same question in mind: what do we do?

Principal Smith and Vice Principal Davis stepped over to World Leader Jordan. Principal Smith accepted the megaphone and let out a faint laugh. "What did we tell you? Expect the unexpected!"

The students glanced at each other.

"What will she tell you and your classmates?" Uri asked Chávez.

"Principal Smith and Vice Principal Davis will try to persuade the students to stay," Chávez stated. "The heads are more concerned about losing their funds than they are about their actual students. See, most of the parents who bring their kids here think that the staff are filthy rich and behave like adopted parents for their kids while they run off and do whatever they want."

Uri and Chávez exchanged glances as the crowd of students shoved each other closer to the academy's boundaries.

"We've allowed our staff to teach you everything to the best of our own knowledge," Principal Smith said with a nervous giggle.

The students nodded and shouted "yes!" as she continued. "Do you also agree that we have provided you with the freedom to feel comfortable with independent decision-making?"

The students agreed again, focused on Principal Smith's earnest speech. "Now, we want you to decide: you may either join World Leader Jordan—her people will provide you with higher quality necessities, such as a better education, food, and clothing, and you will live in a completely safe environment—or you may remain with us, and you will study and work under the harsh conditions at the academy. I will not sugarcoat it. We do not have the advantages that World Leader Jordan has." She stretched out her arms. "If you want to stay with us, stay behind the academy's boundaries; if you want to leave, stand by World Leader Jordan."

The students shifted according to Principal Smith's instructions. Uri noticed that Chávez remained behind the fence, watching as everyone else took part in the separation.

Once the last of the students had made their decisions, World Leader Jordan took a good look at her crowd and then at the academy's crowd before shouting, "We've outnumbered you, Smith and Davis! Let that be a less..."

A sharp screech pierced the sky and a silence fell over

the crowd. Uri guided her eyes to the top of the rain forest and saw a swarm of bats assemble in a tornado shape. Their screeches increased in volume, as they dived toward the academy, knocking branches and smaller animals out of the trees, and leaving a circular space in the middle of the forest.

The ten-foot-long bats circled the sky above the academy. Snipers positioned themselves in the holes of the academy's walls, and half of the guards moved into the formation of a perfect rectangle. The LIES Military stayed on the ground outside of the academy's borders ready to fire.

Uri, World Leader Jordan, and Márquez remained still as the bats performed a series of unpredictable patterns. The bats would glide away from the academy and dip into the forest, swoop upward into a funnel shape in the sky, split into two groups, and then reverse the process. Or they would create an entirely new pattern, which consisted of the bats flying in a helix formation, twisting with each signal they conducted through sonar. The bats then let out sharp shrieks at each other and sped for the academy's main office while remaining in the helix shape. When they appeared distracted, one of the soldiers shouted, "Fire!"

The snipers alternated between firing and observing the bats as their wings constantly adjusted in order to skillfully maneuver during the attacks.

A third of the bats attacked the roofs of the academy's buildings, scratching away at the concrete like a shovel into dry sand. The academy guards opened fire, and the swarm

changed their calls to a symphony of shrieks as they continued to destroy the roofs.

The bats dodged each bullet by flying up into the sky and
then hurling themselves toward the academy. Their bodies
hit the walls with such a powerful strike that the walls vis-
ibly shook.

Some of the bats were missing half of their face; whether it was the left side or the right side varied on each bat.
Their wings spread out to a full twenty feet as they glided
into the skyscraper, creating long tears in the steel structure as if the bats were can openers against an aluminum
structure.

"What are these things?" Márquez shouted at Uri.

Uri could barely get a decent look at the bats without
the remains of a bat spilling over the buildings in a flurry of
brown fur and dark red blood. The bats shrieked to one another at the scent of their deceased companions and then
flew up the front of the main building and darted inside
the air vents. The chink of small bodies smacking against
the ventilation caused some of the younger students to run
deeper into the academy.

Uri turned to Márquez. "Is there anyone inside who is
extremely vulnerable to the bats' attacks?"

"I'm on it!" one of the instructors shouted as she ran
inside the main entrance.

Márquez pointed toward Uri and then to the academy's
entrance. "Go with her! She's going to the nursery on the
right side of this corridor!"

Uri nodded and turned to follow. She felt her head jolt and looked down to see her feet being lifted off the ground. She looked up in horror as she realized that a bat had her in its grip. She watched the academy shrink as the bat took off into the sky. Uri looked up as she and the bat brushed through the muggy air. The bat then grabbed both of her legs as it picked up speed.

"No, please, no," Uri begged as the bat flew higher. "Please let me go."

The bat chirped as if speaking to her and unleashed her from its grip.

Uri found herself screeching the entire way down, waiting for death once she hit the hard ground. But she found herself in a pair of very thin arms, almost like bones. She looked up at the skull of a maned wolf surrounded by orange fur.

"Hello," the creature said in a smooth but unsettling voice.

CHAPTER 9

The creature loomed over Uri. She leaned back to try to avoid staring into her empty black eye sockets and accidentally fell out of the maned wolf's arms onto the dirt floor. She lay on the ground, only paying attention to the rest of the maned wolf's skull. Her permanent fanged grin unleashed an eerie chill into the once muggy rain forest air.

"You seem lost," she said, her teeth unleashing a clicking noise similar to that of a large insect with each word she spoke. "I am Alondra, and I will be your guide."

Uri gently nodded and looked up to the treetops, gripping the tall grass in her hands. The bats that picked her up from the academy gently nestled in the ash-colored branches, their golden eyes glittering like stars in the shadows. She looked back to Alondra and scratched her head. "Y-you're a guide? Like a spirit?"

"No," Alondra said and laughed. "I am the caretaker of the animals of Earth and will guide you through this new earth."

Alondra extended her arm with her hand spread out. Uri bit her lower lip in hesitation. She wondered if this situation was similar to when she met her first survivor, Quick, who was only interested in selling her her own base.

Before she could reach for Alondra's hand, a bat that was roughly the size of Uri gripped onto the reddish fur on Alondra's arm. Alondra drew her arm back, completely engulfed by the bat.

"You've grown since I last saw you," Alondra chuckled. The bat responded through gentle squeaks and climbed up her arm to cuddle between her bony jaw and the muscle and bone of her shoulder.

Uri turned away to try to disguise her failed introduction by attempting to attract a nearby doe. The doe was timid upon approach, treading the forest floor with her head down. She gently lifted her eyes to Uri, and a third eyelid opened revealing a large black pupil surrounded by a violet iris that took up almost all of her forehead. Uri flinched as the doe pushed her head into her hand and allowed Uri to gently rub her fingertips along the top of the doe's head. She emitted a low purring noise, similar to a cat's, and Uri stepped back, watching as the doe ambled beneath the bushes to rest in the shade.

Uri slowly turned to watch the subtle sway of the plant life caused by the doe nibbling on a nearby bush. The gentle setting of the forest gave Uri a unique sense of tranquility.

She watched as Alondra reached up and plucked a handful of aqua leaves and lowered her hand in front of the doe. The doe gently nibbled on the leaves.

Alondra looked to the treetops and watched as several

large bats flew in from the blue sky toward the reunion she shared with the young bat. She welcomed each bat by a specific name while placing the palm of her hand against each one's forehead.

How can she tell which bat is which? Uri wondered as she stared at the bats.

"Ah!" Alondra exclaimed. "You want to know about my bats."

"Sure," Uri said.

"As well as my other animals?" Alondra asked.

Uri nodded and wanted to ask Alondra if she created or modified the bats with specific names or instincts in mind.

"Human."

Uri snapped out of her trance and turned her head back to Alondra, who tilted her head in awe. "What is your name?"

"Uri," she said. She became distracted by a seven-inch-long black bat with a turquoise gloss along its fur and completed her sentence in a hypnotized voice. "Sergeant Davida Uri."

Uri held out her arm, allowing the bat to grip her jacket sleeve and hang upside down with a carefree expression on its face. She looked up to the deeper shadows of the rain forest where animals that were classified as predators rested to escape the scorching heat of the sun. There were no nearby carcasses, and the predators were completely clean from any traces of a hunt.

"What do the animals eat here?" Uri asked. Her voice

trailed away as she searched for the telltale signs of a hunt. Perhaps Alondra was able to keep the entire forest spotless before tracking another victim for his zoo of rejected or simply strange animals.

"I altered these creatures to be vegetarians," Alondra said. "I possess that power."

Uri thought about how she could respond to Alondra's answer. *How can predators not feel hungry? What about helping humans? If there are no predators, how will humans eat? Will the humans eat the plants?*

"How are you able to keep up with the needs of each animal?" she asked.

"It's not easy." Alondra lowered her head again, a hint of sadness touching the tip of her sentence. "I've been forced to watch sacrifices be made on a daily basis. Some animals end up passing away due to poor genetics, others are due to being unable to find good food sources."

Uri pondered Alondra's words as she carried on with her story.

"As much as I do not want to watch my animals devour each other, it may be necessary for them to survive," Alondra twitched at her own response and continued climbing along the trees. "Well, I've told you everything I know about myself. I want to hear about you: What kind of species are you? Where did you come from?"

Uri looked up to the sky, thinking about Shamayim and its civilians.

"It's a long story."

CHAPTER 10

Alondra clicked her fangs together while processing Uri's prolonged explanation of Shamayim. "So that's why you're here."

Uri nodded and noticed a toucan cleaning its fuchsia and teal feathers while perched on the nearby trunk of a fallen palm tree. The toucan hopped onto Uri's shoulder as the two passed by, and its feathers brushed over Uri's jacket while one maroon feather bobbed over its head.

"Hopefully," Uri said softly as the toucan delicately rested its head against her cheek, "Earth will be completely restored for everyone on Shamayim."

"You would allow abusive humans like that to dwell on this beautiful planet?" Alondra said as she gritted her teeth together in panic, "Are you insane?"

"I can see why you would be worried," Uri said. The toucan let out a squawk and hopped onto a star-shaped berry bush.

"Yes, yes," Alondra nodded. "If your kind is as bad as you say it is, you are not fit to take domain over Earth."

"Not all humans are terrible," Uri replied. "We still try to find ways to maintain a healthy Earth."

Alondra pulled herself away quickly to tend to two three-headed tigers lounging by a water hole. She motioned for Uri to approach the two tigresses and pointed at another bush containing more of the star-shaped berries. "Only feed the tigers from that bush. You are looking for dark purple and white swirls on the berries, and the berries must be the same size as the tigress's entire eye."

Uri plucked a handful of the berries and sifted through the small pile, gently holding up one of the berries to the first tiger's face.

"Are these berries edible for humans?" Uri asked as she brought her hands full of berries up to both of the tigers' heads and watched as they snacked away at the pieces of fruit.

"They are if you want severe diarrhea for a full twelve hours," Alondra said earnestly.

Uri refrained from tasting the berries and proceeded to feed the tigresses. The tigresses lapped up every last berry until Uri's hands were completely clean. Then they licked the purple juice stain off of their lips. Uri went to pick more berries as she listened to Alondra.

"So explain this to me, Uri," Alondra said cautiously. "Why would your kind even want to try to 'restore' Earth? Obviously, Earth is beyond what your kind would consider inhabitable. Even I don't know what caused this destruction, and I have never met any of your kind to receive a full understanding in order to make a fair judgment."

Uri carefully allowed Alondra's words to roll around

inside of her mind before admitting, "I'm not sure why, really; it was a mission from my commanders."

"Your commanders are fine with you being here?" Alondra hissed. "Do they know about the new life on Earth?"

"No," Uri hesitated.

Alondra murmured to herself as she went to tend to a variety of snakes resting in a tree.

Uri idly watched as Alondra held up a handful of the same berries, and the snakes devoured them.

"Alondra, do you ever plan to restore Earth? I mean, you already take care of the wildlife. Why not care for humans as well?"

Uri flinched as Alondra leaned forward into her face and let out a low hiss. "Weren't you listening? I said that I do not want your kind returning to the caretakers' territories and destroying all of the beautiful wildlife!" Alondra finished with a shout that sent animals scattering away from where the two stood.

Uri looked down at the berries in her hands. She nearly crushed them, causing the purple juice to stain her dirt-coated hands. She quickly dropped the berries in front of the tigress and murmured a brief "okay."

As Uri approached one of the bushes to gather more berries, she caught Alondra tapping her finger against her jaw in thought. She stopped to listen to what Alondra would say next.

"I might...allow only you to stay," Alondra hesitated as she knelt down to gather more berries.

Uri stared at Alondra. "No, I want all humans to live on Earth. Is that really too much to ask?"

Alondra took a breath through her nostrils. She shoved the rest of the berries into the tigress's mouth and stood back as it sprayed juice at her.

"Come, Sergeant," Alondra said, "it is time to take care of the fish."

Uri dropped the rest of her berries in front of the tiger, and its three heads fought to devour the fruit.

Uri followed Alondra to a murky river. Animals left behind tiny ripples as they darted beneath the surface of the river. "The creatures of the water do not like to be touched; gently crawl to the edge of the river and carefully toss in the berries."

That will be easy, Uri sighed sarcastically as she snatched the berries from Alondra's hand. She walked toward the river and knelt at the edge of the land, where she looked down at her cloudy reflection in the water. Tiny ripples from the fish's fins broke the surface of her reflection as she let the first berry drop from her hand into the river. The fish huddled together. Three of the colorful river creatures poked their heads out of the water, and Uri let a few more berries drop from her hand.

A tiny ripple formed directly beneath her arm. Uri brought her hand closer to the surface and opened it to release more of the berries. She watched as a long, thin reddish creature reached up and wrapped around her wrist. Her head jerked as the top half of her body was yanked forward.

She opened her eyes to see a silhouette of a thin serpent-like creature rapidly swim toward her. She felt something pull on her as she tried to lift her head out of the water. Something that looked like rope lodged into the river's floor was hooked around her wrist. She loosened the rope and cringed as she felt something slimy smack against the side of her face and hook onto her ear.

Uri felt Alondra's large hand pull her up by her shoulder and throw her onto the shore. She gasped as she wiped the water and mud from her eyes with the drier parts of her sleeves. Her head tilted from side to side as she tried to steady it.

"Sergeant!" Alondra gasped, "are you all right?"

Uri felt a thick substance gather deeper into her right ear canal. She tilted her head, groaning as steady drops of water exited her ear followed by a whisper. Uri scratched her ear, listening as the whispers grew louder, before stopping. Uri looked up at Alondra whose permanent skeleton grin showed great concern.

"All done," she said and she smiled at Alondra.

Alondra appeared shocked. "You're alright? Incredible! Come, we have so much more to do today!"

CHAPTER 11

Alondra searched through the overgrowth of the rain forest, stopping at every fruit tree to examine the brown and orange lizards that crawled along the branches. She allowed five lizards to crawl onto her arm and muttered either "yes" or "no."

"What I will teach you today," Alondra said as she held a tiny black lizard with orange speckles up to Uri, "is how to detect certain diseases on different animals."

Uri tried to appear interested, yet her mind wandered. She was running a finger along the concha of her right ear when a ringing noise pulsated throughout her brain. The noise increased for a brief second and then decreased back to a soft whisper. She pushed the palms of her hands against both ears as the ringing traveled to both sides.

"Do you hear that, Alondra?" Uri asked while turning in what she believed was the direction of the noise. However, everything went silent.

Alondra stopped to listen as well. A breeze swept through the treetops followed by the relaxing tweets of tiny dark green birds tending to their newborns.

Uri scratched her ear, and the ringing turned into a

high-pitched screech. "God!" Uri shouted. She pressed her hands harder against her head and dropped to her knees.

Alondra hurried to Uri's side and removed her hands from her ears.

"Can you not hear that?" Uri shouted, and the nearby animals fled the scene. The ringing stopped, and Uri frantically looked around.

The forest in Uri's sight turned into a blurry mess of greens, grays, and blues. The trees closest to her took the shape of gray rectangles while Alondra and the rest of the rain forest faded away. The ground beneath Uri's feet slowly vanished into a shallow pool of a gray liquid.

"Alondra?" Uri shouted while looking around frantically. She thought she could hear the chattering noise Alondra made with her teeth. Uri walked forward as her shouting slowly subsided, and she muttered, "Are you still there?"

A sharp sting shot through Uri's brain. She grabbed her head and groaned in pain while leaning her body against the closest solid surface she could feel. She looked up to see another one of the gray rectangles take shape. A nauseating feeling clouded her mind, and then she heard the voice of a young man.

"Hello in there," the voice stretched out the word at the end of its greeting.

Uri's vision became blurry again, and the voice continued, "My name is..."—static filled Uri's head in place of the voice—"and I am here to help you."

"I'm sure you are," Uri murmured as she rubbed her

eyes and her blurry vision faded to black.

The voice unleashed static inside Uri's head again, which sent another sharp sting through her brain, "Why do you follow that caretaker?" The voice laughed, "She will never help you, at least, not like we will help you."

Another voice, one of a little girl, let out a short chuckle before taking on a serious tone. "There is a very special place at the edge of this rain forest. I will lead you there."

"No," Uri responded in a tired voice. "I will not tolerate this crap."

She turned in the direction she had come from, and the high-pitched screech sounded again. Uri covered her ears with her hand. She hissed as her body crumpled onto the ground.

"I just told you that you will go to the edge of the rain forest, and you will obey me," said a voice belonging to a man in his midthirties.

"How do I know you won't get me killed?" Uri asked.

"You can trust us, Sergeant Uri," a voice resembling one of the world leaders said softly. "We promise we won't hurt you."

"I'll humor you," Uri said and followed the voices' demand. She felt a thick substance similar to mud slosh to both sides of her head. She knelt down on the reflective black ground and saw her irises change from a dark brown to a foggy gray. She watched her reflection as she lifted her hand to scratch where the voices started. As her fingertip touched the edge of her ear canal, she felt a sharp pain shoot through her skin. Uri hissed as she brought the finger back to her face. Maroon slime molded over her fingertip where a tiny bite mark could be seen.

She walked along to the voices' commands without control over her own mind.

"Go right," a voice on the left side whispered.

"No, go left!" a voice on the right side snapped.

"Stop!" both voices boomed.

Uri looked up at a two-story studio apartment with a large sign on the roof reading "Charline Traverse's Photography Studio." Moss covered the outside.

"Go inside!" the voices ordered.

Uri snapped out of her trance and opened the door. Inside was a waiting room lined with a variety of seating, from plastic lawn chairs to bar stools, next to end tables topped with magazines.

The voices then whispered, "Look behind that door."

Uri felt her body being turned to face another door across from the main entrance. This door was opened to a hallway where she could see the Shadow. The Shadow from before ran through the hallway, opening doors and carrying various types of photography equipment back and forth between rooms.

Inside, Uri was blinded by a black-and-white checked floor that clashed with the walls of pink and blue swirls. She looked down at one of the most surprising objects she had seen since the books at the academy: stacks of magazines with a sign above them that said, "Yes, I do everything old-fashioned. Get over it."

She gently lifted the corner of one magazine and let each page drop, listening as the papers gently landed on each other.

Uri looked to the front desk on the other side of the room. The desk kept a wall calendar containing the names and dates of clients. To the right of the calendar was a flatscreen computer that had lost popularity when communicators first hit the markets.

A snapping sound could be heard in the distance. Uri looked down the hall that led to a staircase connecting the first and second floors. She crept upstairs, listening for any changes in sounds.

The only items occupying the second floor were a projector showing samples of the images and a desk with a notebook and a cup of writing tools. The slide opened with a business logo and the years of the photo sessions, then moved on to the sample images. One photo depicted a couple at their wedding, the next was a family portrait, and another was a graduation photo.

Uri squinted at the images to pick up on subtle details. In the wedding photo, the colors in the background bled together and dripped across the couple's faces; the family was covered in cuts and bruises in the portrait, and a coffin could be seen in the background of the graduation photo. The slide changed to a typical photograph of a soldier standing in a wheat field, smiling at the camera. Upon a second look, Uri recognized the face; it was hers.

The slideshow ceased. Uri looked to the back of the room where the projector sat in cobwebs on top of the desk.

"Go to the projector," the voices whispered.

Uri attempted to calmly respond to the voices, "Why do I—"

"Go, you idiot!" one of the voices shouted.

Uri flinched and covered her ears, as the shout ended with a long ringing sound before the whispers continued, combined with deep murmurs.

Uri quietly obeyed and slipped behind the desk. The machine was similar to the holographic technology on Shamayim, only its keypad was connected to the monitor and it could fold inward after being turned off.

Uri tapped the square pad beneath the keyboard with her index finger. As she moved her finger, the slideshow closed out to a photo gallery. She selected the gallery's icon and scrolled through the queue until she reached the photograph of herself in the wheat field.

Her image maintained eye contact with the camera and held a relaxed, closed-lipped smile as though she was aware that her picture was being taken. However, she had no recollection of the event, nor was she familiar with a photographer named Charline Traverse. Not only that, but the sky was a light blue as opposed to its current green color, which meant the photo would have been taken prior to the Mysterious War and before she was even born. She zoomed in and out in search of anything that might provide clues to the Mysterious War or to the Hawkinses, whoever they were.

She clicked to the next photograph where she remained in the same location, only now she was sitting in the grass with her legs crossed. When she saw no changes in the background, she clicked on the next picture where she was standing again.

Uri hunted through the desk for any information on these strange photographs. She opened the top drawer, which revealed an object that resembled the "books" at the academy. "Journal" was printed in gold lettering on the front of the green leaf-print cover, which had large creases along the spine. She flipped to the first page, a simple intro- duction with a signature from the writer.

December 1, 2089

Dear Diary,

Just won a bunch of vintage technology from a couple of online auctions! Can't wait to start Charline Traverse's Vintage Photog- raphy Studio!

Charline

Uri looked up to see another photograph of herself in the same position, only this time a woman with pale skin, visible veins, and clothing constructed from sackcloth stood on her right side. She nodded with caution and turned to the next page of Charline's journal.

December 20, 2089

Dear Diary,

First customers! Forgot their names; got to check customer re-cords!

Until tomorrow!

Charline

How do you forget your very first customers? Uri thought and looked back to the slideshow. This time, a man with a similar appearance to the woman stood on the left side in Uri's photograph. Both the man and the woman had crazy looks in their eyes as they glared at Uri. She turned back to read Charline's next diary entry.

December 21, 2089

Dear Diary,

Checked the couple's photographs. The images contained strange details. Shadows that shouldn't be there are in the frame, lighting is dimmer than what I meant it to be, and chunks of the photo are blurry. That's right, chunks! Checked my order forms and I have absolutely no records of the couple ever coming to my studio. I can't even remember their names. Creepy!

Charline

Uri checked the slideshow again. The man and woman's

faces had turned sullen, and their entire bodies stood next to Uri in the photograph. The slide shifted to the next photograph, where the woman had her arm positioned to deliver a blow to Uri's throat. Uri showed no signs of acknowledging that the woman was about to hit her. The next photograph depicted Uri's body on the ground, surrounded by a dead wheat field and the couple standing over her. The next five photographs showed the man stomping on Uri's head while the woman punched Uri's ribs.

The next photograph showed the couple glaring at their results. Uri's flesh had faded to an unusual pale color, causing the streaks of blood to stand out along her body; her swollen eyes blocked her vision; and some of her broken bones stuck out of her flesh.

"What is that supposed to mean?" Uri questioned as she broke out in sweat. She referred to Charline's diary again.

December 24, 2089

Dear Diary,

Things have been going wrong for me. My equipment has been crapping out before its time, my pictures look like my first clients' photographs, and I've received nothing but lawsuits and lost customers.

Merry Christmas to me!

Charline

Uri looked at the next photo. The man and woman were looking directly into the camera. Their furious glares burned into Uri's brain. She gripped the back of her neck when she felt a wave of heat hit it. She started to believe that the man and woman were standing right behind her.

A thick liquid trickled down Uri's forehead. She ran her finger across her temples and pulled them away to see blood stain her flesh. She ran her fingertips across her neck where a deep bruise was located in the photograph, and she flinched. She needed to leave before things became worse.

She placed Charline's journal and her communicator in her backpack, clinging to the hope that her recordings could provide more clues to almost anything—the Hawkinses, Alondra, the academy.

Uri's thoughts again were interrupted by the clicking noise in her head. This time a gentle flow of chirps were added to the noise. Unfortunately, those sounds were followed by a montage of gruesome images flooding her mind. One image depicted an unclean butcher shop; another depicted the couple from the images covered in blood. The chirping ceased, and one of the voices gently sang, "Hello, Davida, we'd like a word with you."

The voices emitted clicking noises in Uri's head. She felt tension build up inside as she prepared to listen to what the voices had to say.

More images of the couple and the butcher shop flooded Uri's mind. Images that followed were of pale-skinned humans, various animals missing half of the flesh on their faces, and sterilized operating tables.

"Are you satisfied with your work?" one voice snarled.

The other voices whispered, "What's the answer?"

Uri tried to ignore the voices by focusing on leaving Charline's studio and opened the door. "Crap!" Uri shouted as memories of the bats at the academy hit her. "The world leaders were in the bat attack."

"What does that matter to you?" another voice whispered in a soothing tone. "We'll be your guides now."

The voices proceeded to collaborate in murmurs. Uri continued walking, only picking up on phrases like "You think so?" or "Good question."

Uri held her head in her hand as she tried to break the agonizing murmurs. "The world leaders were not my guides…"

"Answer us!" an elderly man's voice boomed over Uri, while the rest of the voices cackled, "Do you feel satisfied? Yes or no?"

Uri hesitated and shut the main entrance to the studio. She concentrated on journeying back into the rain forest, hoping it would keep the voices out of her head.

She set off in a random direction. Uri took the best road since the voices did not become combative. Rain splashed onto the large leaves and filled the nearby swamps. Uri considered confusing the voices by counting the number of raindrops or humming some unfamiliar song.

"We can see your thoughts!" a high-pitched voice sang, "and we do not care for your answers!"

Uri's plan failed.

The voices resorted to murmuring with their only audible words being "yes" or "no."

"Why did that caretaker of the earth take you in?" a stern voice asked. "She hates humans."

Uri's mind wandered to Alondra. Would Alondra search for her, or would Alondra have returned to tending to her animals? "Alondra is going to kill me."

"What's Alondra got to do with any of this?" a young boy's voice asked. "You listen to us."

"Why are you even here?" a female's baritone voice sang, accompanied by snickers. "Don't your leaders use you as a pawn?"

Uri pushed her fingers into her temples. She came to the edge of the land, where a murky river split her path from the next island. She tried to direct her thoughts to anything other than the voices.

"Job satisfaction?" The voice of a teenage girl laughed. "You don't have it!"

Uri let out a shout of frustration. "How can you read all of that?"

She increased her speed by taking large strokes across the river and climbed up onto the next island. The voices carried out their inaudible chattering, leaving her in the dark about what they were carefully plotting.

"You hate humans," the voice of a young man whispered, "right?"

"What?" Uri twitched. "No!"

"Oh, come on now!" The voices laughed. "Humans are selfish, crude, and manipulative, even that caretaker knows that!"

The voices reverted to clicking noises. The clicks began to resemble rapid ticking noises, similar to a time bomb. A low growl vibrated through Uri's head followed by the voice of a small child that said, "Even the world leaders know that."

Uri shook her head. She hiked along the sandy mound, watching as animals backed out of her path and into the tall grass and shadows. The voices twisted inside of Uri's brain, as if digging for memories to use against what actually occurred in that memory.

"Aren't you exhausted from the insanity of it all?" the voice of a business woman barked. "The loneliness? The ignorance? The drama?"

Uri wiped sweat and mud off of her forehead with her cleaner hand. She was failing to conjure up clever responses to the voices in her head and, more so, ideas about how she could get rid of them.

"Listen, Sergeant Uri," a voice similar to World Leader Jordan said, "we exist to serve you."

The words echoed throughout the rain forest. Uri gathered thousands of words to produce her response to this unanticipated statement. However, the only word that fell from her lips was "How?"

"We'll serve as your advocates," answered a voice replicating her father's. "We'll bring your most important thoughts to your attention, and you simply speak our words. Like we said, we'll be your guides."

Uri felt her mind become cloudy. The scenery turned to gray. Her nervous system felt tighter, and she lost control of movement. She used the last of her willpower to look at her feet. The voices caused her to move in a typical fashion. Her arms hung at her side, her back remained straight, and she kept a casual speed as she walked.

"Don't worry," a young girl's voice whispered, "we've done this before."

Uri felt she was growing vulnerable to the sounds of the voices. She tilted her head to the ground, trying to use what little pieces of her mind she had to make sure she did not trip on any tree roots or uneven earth. Her feet made gentle crunches against the mud until she heard her boots step on metal. She looked down to see a manhole cover labeled "City Sewer."

"Why is there a city sewer in the middle of a rain forest?" Uri asked herself.

"Let's check it out!" squeaked a cheerful voice, followed by the encouraging chants from the other voices.

Uri pulled off the cover of the manhole, and the voices became silent. She leaned forward to look down into the seemingly bottomless hole while her heart raced. Suddenly a humanlike wail echoed throughout the sewer system.

CHAPTER 12

Uri kept a firm grip on the bars as she climbed into the sewer system. The wailing rose again causing the entire sewer to shake. The lid slowly crept over the manhole with each vibration, until it settled into its place and the sunlight was completely cut off. The shaking ceased, yet the wailing continued.

Uri jumped down from the ladder, and her feet hit the murky water, causing sewer rats to scatter away from the rotten chunks of food that littered the walkways. Dead rats and pieces of garbage floated with the current, while drops of earthy water leaked between the cracks in the walls, and rats scurried to lap up the clean water of the day.

A pack of rats, ranging from six to eight inches in length, followed a single nine-inch-long rat along the pipes. The rat acknowledged Uri's presence and let out a sharp squeak that caused the sewer pipes to shake. It then continued to scurry along the pipes while the rest of the rats followed closely behind.

Uri's head throbbed as one of the voices bounced against her brain in order to catch her attention.

"What was that noise?" the voice of a female child whispered.

"Alien, demon, ghost," the voice of a male teenager responded. "Whatever you want it to be."

"What about the rats?" Uri asked. "Are they anything that should scare me?"

"Silence!" the voices shouted.

Uri grew quiet and allowed the voices to carry out their directions through the sewer. The voices chattered among themselves, stating their predictions regarding what the source of the wailing was, and they resorted to murmuring out directions. The voices whispered, "Turn left."

Uri felt her feet drag along the concrete as she was forcefully guided in the voices' desired directions.

"Turn right," the voices muttered. Uri was guided down a tunnel covered in a rainbow of profane graffiti. One voice murmured about the ideal fall of humans, and Uri's entire body flipped, causing her to land on her back. She was pinned to the floor. The voices snickered as they allowed Uri to stand.

"I currently find you more obnoxious than helpful." Uri rolled her eyes. "And humans are not that bad."

The voices thrusted themselves toward the frontal lobe of Uri's brain. Uri gripped her head in response to the intense headache that followed. The voices unleashed another series of shrieks, causing Uri to fall to her knees. The colors in the scenery around her became unsaturated. The pitch-black voids grew lighter, revealing the walkways next to the sewer walls. The shallow and deep sections of the sewer became more pronounced through a contrast of light greens.

"I believe that we've won that argument," the voice of the elderly man hissed.

"Davida." The voice replicating her father spoke again. "We will guide you, but you must trust us."

Uri rose to her feet. The voices' murmurs echoed in her head and traveled along her nervous system. A red fog leaked into the sewer system through the many cracks in the walls and pipes, and the layout of the sewer shifted. Materials varying from paper to scrap metal flickered in and out of existence. The walls rotated clockwise, and black vines twisted along with the new trail that was taking formation. Uri twitched when the vines subtlety crept toward her and gripped her arms and legs.

"Do not worry," the voice of Uri's mother sang. "We'll get out of this alive."

Uri asked in a shaky voice, "Are you in control of all of this?"

"Of course," the voice of Uri's father replied, "but we are only showing you what we want you to see."

Uri's mind faded in and out of reality. She attempted to walk forward until her vision slowly faded and the voices fully took over. She blinked, and the murky green and rust colors of the sewer turned to gray.

"You panic because you do not allow us to control you," the female child said. "We need to be in control so you will have a clear mind."

Uri felt her energy abandon her physical body and the voices completely take possession. She took one last look at her reflection in the sewer water. Her irises changed from a cloudy gray to a light blue, and her flesh grew pale. The voices nested deeper into her mind, creating light chuckles.

"We're not entirely certain what your destination is," the teenager's voice added. "However, we can see that you are attempting to locate some form of..." The teenager's voice trailed off. It slowly grew louder and then faded to a whisper of the word "interesting."

A low rumble crept along the ground. Pipes clinked and busted one at a time while the rats leaped onto the walkway and huddled together. The rats lined up along the pipes and edges around the sewer tunnels.

"Just turn around," the teenager's voice spoke again. "They'll leave you alone."

When Uri hesitated, the voices repossessed her body. The void overtook the sewer.

"Like we said," the voice of Uri's father added, "we will be your guides."

Uri's body was taken back to the dimension that consisted of gray rectangles. A path of glass stepping-stones formed into a downward spiral. Uri cautiously stepped onto the first stone, and the stone moved down within an inch of the next stone. She leaped off of the stone and onto the next stone until she automatically moved from one stone to another.

"Stop!" the female child commanded.

A rectangle floated upward in front of Uri and vertically split apart, taking the shape of a ladder leading up to another manhole cover. Uri found herself back in the sewer system.

The voices chattered among each other again, and the voice of the female child piped up, "We're here!"

The voices unleashed their grip from Uri's nervous system, granting her control over her body again. Uri's eyes twitched as the voices squished around her brain before holing back into the corner of it. She looked up the sewer's rusty ladder. The words "Your Destination: Hell," along with an arrow pointing up to the manhole cover, were painted on the wall in yellow spray paint.

"Those words mean nothing," the voice of the child said and laughed. "Keep going!"

The wailing rose again, this time sounding closer. Uri pushed away the manhole cover and climbed up onto the asphalt outside. She quickly pushed the lid back over the manhole, silencing the wails. The wails echoed in her mind as they grew distant under the manhole cover. Uri hyperventilated when the wails collided with the whispers of the voices. She used one hand to massage her temples and the other to block the sunlight that appeared to be much more intense than usual.

"Those noises cannot be that obnoxious." An alto voice laughed. "They will never hurt you."

"I don't want to be the test subject of your theory," Uri

hissed as she placed a pair of sunglasses over her eyes and waited for her migraine to die down. Unfortunately, her migraine was replaced with a sharp pain that shot throughout her nervous system.

"Silence!" the alto voice boomed. "You're here."

Uri tried to force herself to focus on her surroundings. When her vision repeatedly shifted from blurry to clear, she grunted out of impatience, "You need to control my vision too?"

"Yes," the voices responded cheerfully.

Uri relaxed her entire body and closed her eyes as the voices swarmed her mind. "Fine, I will no longer fight you," she murmured. "Show me what you need me to see."

"Look around you," the voice of Uri's father whispered, "but do not remove your sunglasses."

Uri opened her eyes. The colors of the objects in her vision changed to vibrant shades that did not match the objects. The sky became an eerie mix of greens and yellows, and the sun changed to a light blue.

A city of skyscrapers encased the area around the manhole. The buildings were made of jagged crystal shapes. Clusters of pebbles formed along the corners of the entrances and roofs of the buildings.

Uri walked forward and flinched at the first object she came upon. Steel cubes were freely suspended over the sidewalks and roads in diagonal patterns. Each cube was spaced out at four feet horizontally and eight feet vertically, allowing Uri the space to walk through the rows. She looked at the buildings and noticed that the cubes parted as they came close to the buildings and took on the same pattern down the alleyways.

"Am I allowed to touch the cubes?" Uri asked as she reached for one of them.

"Stand back and watch," the voices said.

A small neon bluebird dropped a feather as it flew through the rows of cubes. The feather gently touched the surface of one of the cubes causing tiny pebble-like bumps to protrude along its corners.

"If you touch the cube again, its pebbles will grow into spikes long enough to impale you," the business woman's voice growled, "which will kill us as well."

"I see no downside to your statement," Uri muttered. The voices unleashed their screams, causing Uri to become tense. She felt one of her arms swing upward and gasped as it almost brushed against one of the cubes.

"Okay!" Uri shouted. "I get it!"

Uri stood back from the cubes and carefully surveyed the city as the voices guided her. She looked back at the cube that the feather had touched to see more pebbles form along its faces.

"Any explanation for the origin of the cubes?" Uri asked the voices.

The voices let out their snickers before one of the more unfamiliar voices responded, "No, we are only using them to set you on a more direct path in order to find survivors."

"Of course," Uri murmured as she maneuvered through

the cubes. "So, let's say, in theory, if someone who was not possessed by you was watching me, they would only see me flailing my arms around an empty space?"

"Yep!" the voices said and let out a roar of laughter. "But the cubes will still impale you; the punishment must fit the crime, you see."

"You're insane," Uri said. "But in order to find the survivors, I will trust you."

Uri watched the floating cubes for any other movement. So far, the cubes remained motionless, and there were currently no other life forms around capable of setting off the cubes.

Uri knelt down to avoid a cube next to her head and looked up. The section of the city she was about to enter did not have the cubes. "I just have a few more feet to go," she whispered.

Uri tilted her head again to avoid another cube, and her eyes darted to her right where a dark humanoid danced along the edge of the final wall of cubes, flailing its arms and legs carelessly. Uri turned her head to the cubes in front of her and then looked back to see that the entity was gone. She turned back toward the edge of the city. "It's not real; nothing is really there."

She looked back again in time to see a two-inch-long finger reach out from the shadows and gently touch one of the cubes.

Uri watched as spikes protruded from the cube, and the finger pulled back into the shadows. The spikes broke through the bottom rows of the cubes, tore into the asphalt, and shattered the windows of vehicles and buildings. Chunks of asphalt and concrete flew to the ground around Uri, leaving potholes. The untouched cubes at the top transformed into spheres, and each one gravitated inches away from the spiky cube, allowing them to produce spikes as well.

Uri looked at the shadows as light poured over the area where she saw the finger reveal an empty alleyway.

The voices faded to murmurs causing the color of Uri's irises to revert to their natural dark brown. Uri blinked rapidly as the scenery changed. The spheres faded out of existence while the natural colors of the city returned. Skyscrapers scrunched down into smaller department stores and apartments. The sky lightened to a natural blue with a bright yellow sun whose light faded in and out with the gentle movement of the soft clouds. A peaceful silence fell over the city, occasionally accompanied by the soft hush of the cool breeze.

Uri pulled up her communicator to stream a video of the city to the LIES leaders. Once she began recording, her hands shook, and a low growl could be heard in the back of her head.

"No, no," the voices shouted, "you need to see what we want to show you!"

Uri's hands opened, letting the communicator fall to pieces on the ground while the voices chanted, "Control!"

Uri then felt something crawling beneath the skin of

her face. She dragged her jagged fingernails down her face, feeling a moist substance touch her hands. She pulled her hands away to see that she had peeled off her flesh in paper-thin pieces, leaving exposed muscle behind. She stared at the pieces of flesh, unsure of what her reaction should be. She dropped the skin to the ground, and the pieces hit the communicator, causing it to reconstruct itself. Uri picked up the communicator in complete awe of its repair.

"Run!" the voices shouted.

Uri looked up to see the spikes pushing deep into the ground and curving upward, bringing the sewer pipes to the surface. The wailing rose from beneath and shook the entire city. Brown water gushed through the space between the manhole and its cover, as well as the drains in the sidewalks, and poured downhill into the streets.

The vibrations shook the ground again, throwing Uri off balance. She looked back at the manhole to see its cover slowly slide off. Uri ran back to the alleyway where she saw the hand and caught a glimpse of a humanoid leap behind the building. The Shadow ran toward the back of the alley and skidded to the right. Uri ran her hand over her forehead when the voices squirmed around.

"You should catch up to that human, Uri!" the voice of the elderly man scolded. "You remember your mission!"

Uri sprinted after the Shadow while calling out, "Wait!" She came to a three-way split in the alley where the Shadow was in the middle of selecting a path. The shadow glanced at Uri and dived down the middle alleyway.

"Wait." Uri shook her head. "That's a human?"

The voices did not respond as they were tied up in an argument over which path Uri needed to take to catch up to the human.

"I say," the voice of World Leader Jordan boomed, "take the right path. You'll catch up to that person much quicker if you're able to intercept it!"

"Are you crazy?" the business woman lashed out. "You don't know what kind of power that thing possesses. You will need to take the center path so it will be surprised, no matter which path it took."

"How will that thing be surprised by us taking the center path?" the female child scoffed. "That's only what it wants us to think so it can kill us! We need to take the left path; it will never suspect the left path."

Uri grew weary as the voices carried out their chaotic argument while ignoring her question, causing her vision to portray the buildings as rows of gray tombstones against a light blue sky. The spheres changed back into cubes and shifted into a row that ran down the road and up toward the sky, separating the two sides of the city.

Pieces of the sidewalk and walls broke off into more cubes, separating Uri from the shadow. Uri ran around to the other side of the building. The alleyway remained brightly lit by the blue sun. The shadows turned to various shades of purple as they stretched out against a pink sidewalk.

Uri looked up to see the shadow leaning casually against a green building. The shadow glanced at Uri and sprinted toward her, slipping past the corner of her eye. Uri turned and chased after it again. She failed to concentrate due to the voices and leaned against the building, pressing her forehead against the concrete.

"Wha-a-t?" the voice of the teenager said in a fake surprised tone. "It escaped! How?"

Uri took a deep breath and returned to the main road. This time the cubes were gone and the colors became normal. She ran her fingers down her face, realizing that her skin had grown back.

"Did you actually think that we would have allowed you to peel your own skin off of your face?" The voices laughed.

Uri ignored them as she hiked along an off-ramp covered in rusted cars and kudzu. She looked down to see white smoke rise over a large forest of pine trees.

"Now," the little girl's voice softened, "what could that be?"

CHAPTER 13

Uri ran her finger along her outer ear. The whispers of the voices multiplied until they resembled the roar of a crowd. She gritted her teeth before shouting, "I am at the point of tearing you out myself!"

A flock of birds scattered from the trees as Uri's echo shot into the distance.

Uri then pulled out her communicator to jot down another tally mark for her time with the voices. She tried sending the recordings to LIES only to receive a notice that the entire base was "closed until further notice."

"Six freaking months." Uri's head twitched. "I have been stuck with a bunch of voices in my head that will not shut up and no specific explanation about where the survivors are."

Uri felt the warmth of the sun fade away. She looked up to see that she was closer to the smokestack. A notification on her communicator alerted her of potential storm reports.

"Warning!" the communicator blared. "Strong winds, showers, and low temperatures are approaching!"

"Could you be more specific?" Uri asked.

The communicator pulled up a loading screen with the

word "Processing" above a green bar. A branch snapped off and smacked into the ground. Uri stood back, and the words "Answer calculated!" flashed across the screen.

"No," the communicator responded in a flat voice and automatically shut off.

"Do you really need to rely on that piece of crap?" The voices laughed. "I would have thrown that communicator into a landfill a long time ago."

"Why?" Uri snapped. "Because you're so dependable?"

The voices let out shrill cries in anger. Uri cringed and covered her ears.

"There is nothing here," the voice of the little girl hissed impatiently. "You should go to the smokestack."

Uri ignored the voice and continued to walk along the highway. So far, the voice was correct. The only signs of life were the crows that landed on the ground to pick at pieces of garbage and gravel, followed by the occasional deer that crossed the road every couple of minutes.

Uri looked around. She could see the Shadow running down the road away from her. As Uri tried to walk toward the Shadow, the voices turned her body toward the opening at the edge of a bright green meadow.

"Go this way," the voices said cheerfully.

Uri looked back to see the Shadow wave its hand at her, beckoning Uri to follow it. Uri turned to try to follow the Shadow, but the voices turned her body back to the meadow.

"Chicken! Chicken!" the voices chanted as Uri stopped

at the edge of a dark forest. The smoke slowly died down as the voices' volume decreased and then grew again as the voices increased.

"Are you causing me to see the smoke just so I can go to it?" Uri yelled.

"Maybe," the voices snickered. The child's voice finished with a giggly response. "But it's only because you need to know where you're going."

Uri felt her body being pulled deeper into the forest. As the trees flew by, she caught the sound of a voice singing in the distance. Her body skidded to a halt where she was placed in a patch of grass in a forest clearing. The smoke vanished, and pieces of moss, leaves, and twigs slithered out of her path. The pieces came together to form a tightly woven female body. The plants wrapped tightly around each other, giving the female a smoother appearance. More plants twisted down her shoulder to form a hand motioning Uri to come to her.

Uri felt the foliage beneath her feet rise up and fling her body forward. She landed on her back and lifted up her head to keep it from hitting the ground. Her eyes opened to meet the five slits that made up the plant formation's face. More foliage twisted into the lower half of the plant formation until the woman was able to stand.

Uri scrambled to her feet and stared up at the woman, estimating that she was the same height as Alondra and was possibly another caretaker. Twigs from a walnut tree extended from her fingertips to the entrance of Uri's ears.

Uri reached up to try to pull her fingers out; however, the woman resisted, and her fingers slithered in deeper before she quickly pulled them out.

A long leech squirmed and shrieked in the woman's hand. She brought the leech up to Uri's face and allowed her to examine it. The six-inch-long leech lunged toward Uri. Its jaw lowered, revealing a bunch of tiny mouths behind a row of razor-sharp teeth. Maroon slime dripped down its cherry red and charcoal-black skin.

Uri looked down at her shoulder as she felt a trail of the slime, mixed with blood and ear wax, drip down the side of her neck.

The woman crushed the leech, and it let out a hissing noise until it turned to soot in her hand. Her lips formed a gentle smile as she said, "Sorry about that; that leech must have been attached to you for quite some time."

She opened her hand releasing the soot with the breeze.

"You do not know the half of it," Uri said as she scratched her ear. She felt a thick liquid on her skin, and she brought up her hand to watch the trail of maroon slime drip down her arm.

She looked around the forest. The smokestack was no longer visible from where she stood. The gray clouds above were still visible, causing light drops to fall over Uri and the caretaker.

"Alondra has told me about you." The caretaker's soothing voice caused the vines along her body to become more radiant. "You came to help us restore Earth."

"You know Alondra?" Uri shouldn't have been surprised since this woman was another eight-foot-tall caretaker who appeared to tend to plant life.

"I should know a fellow caretaker," she responded. "I am Liana, and I take care of the Earth's plant life."

The tightly woven plant life that Liana was constructed of settled to an unusual shade of green, causing the trees around them to turn the same rich color. Warm sunlight peaked through the spaces in the tree branches. A patch of light green grass perked up and swayed as if it could reach up and touch them. Liana ran her hand through the grass, and it returned to its dark green state.

Uri looked down at the grass. As she reached down to feel the area that Liana restored, she flinched and pulled her hand back as she watched the once luscious grass dry out again. She looked up to see that Liana had her back turned to her as she placed her hand on some sagebrush, and its dying yellow flowers perked up with life.

Uri nervously eyed the flowers and decided not to touch them. She looked back at Liana who was separating strands of tangled grass.

"So, Liana," Uri said, "how did Alondra let you know that she knew me?"

"She sent me a message via one of her birds." Liana studied her finished product of well-kept grass. "She claimed that you're the only human who does not attempt to destroy everything. Come, we have so much to do!"

Wild flowers bloomed as Liana pulled Uri deeper into

the field. The flowers leaned toward Liana as she passed through but then fell away as Uri brushed past them. Uri looked up as Liana sat on the grass, gently brushing her fingers up the blades and watching as they perked up again.

She asked Uri if she had traveled to the other countries in the world, what they were like, if the other caretakers were okay, and if there were more of her kind there. Uri recalled her conversation with Alondra and decided to only bring up the better side of humans so Liana would at least show her species some grace.

"Sergeant Uri," Liana said as she plucked the fungus off of a tree, "how do you manage your species? Surely you provide them with rules."

"Rules?" Uri said. "No, I don't provide the rules."

"Oh, of course!" Liana laughed. "Caretakers are not meant to provide rules. Silly me, we are meant to take care of life on Earth, not burden them with unnecessary rules! So, how do you take care of the human beings?"

"Liana, no," Uri said. "I'm trying to find survivors. I'm not here to help you restore Earth."

"What do you mean?" Liana asked with a hint of anger in her voice.

Uri looked down to see Liana's feet change from a glowing green to a dull brown. The green grass around her feet died and spread to the rest of the forest. The wild flowers shriveled up.

"I really don't know," Uri said as she watched flower stems curl down into the dirt.

Liana rolled her eyes and fell backward onto the ground with a huff. The plants surrounding her wrapped around her body. "You humans are too complicated," she said.

"Liana, please listen," Uri said, but she was cut off as Liana waved her hand.

"Take a break," she said. "I got a headache from listening to you."

"Wait, Liana." Uri wanted to argue but stopped when Liana closed her eyes and covered her ears with her hands. Her flesh darkened to match the greens of the field until she was practically camouflaged. Uri figured it was time to leave her alone when Liana started snoring.

She looked up to the base of the forest and saw the Shadow running.

"Liana?" Uri murmured and ran back to where Liana lay fast asleep on her back with her arms crossed over her chest. Uri quietly walked away when she realized that Liana had no more information about the Mysterious War or the red and black leeches. She wanted to make it up to Liana for rescuing her from the leech inside of her ear.

"I should probably wait until Liana consults Alondra, since Alondra trusts me more," Uri said to herself.

She wandered away from Liana's meadow. The rainbow of flowers and green grass twisted into light brown weeds and thorns. The leaves rustled beneath Uri's feet, and she looked up to see the split where Liana's lively green forest ended.

Uri heard the cracking of plastic. She looked beneath her

feet to see a broken sign peeking through the grass. It read, "McKenna's Family Farm" with an arrow pointing downhill. Uri looked to see a two-story, cube-shaped, cream-colored house at the bottom of the hill next to a two-story red barn. Uri climbed down and slid into a wooden corral at the edge of the hill. She peered over the top rail of the corral to see a hen at the foot of a chicken coop, slowly opening and closing her eyes. She gently folded her wing back revealing a dozen chicks that appeared to have recently died.

Uri looked over to a second corral and saw a rabbit that seemed to have been dead for a couple of hours. She looked in the other corrals to see that the animals were either sick or dead. Some were also missing pieces of their bodies.

Uri walked toward the house to see if someone was home. Shadows of people moved rapidly behind the curtains. A loud thump sounded against the wall, and the curtain slipped off of the rod. Taking up most of the window, a large television screen with dents and cracks could be seen. Uri crouched until her eyes were just below the television, and she stared, mouth agape.

Three pale-skinned humanlike beings occupied the room. Each of the beings had purple veins visible against their pale flesh. Their heads were covered in a strange, transparent, slimy maroon substance that dripped down their bodies.

One being sat behind the window Uri was looking through. It leaned back in an easy chair with its sharp, untrimmed fingernails tearing into the fabric, causing the stuffing to fall out. A second being stood over the first, scolding in gibberish and shaking its finger at the first. It proceeded to point to the television where Uri now noticed a crowbar lying in front of it. Uri ducked, keeping her eyes just above the television's stand and continued to spy on this new group of beings.

She pulled her communicator out to record the beings' actions. She focused on a third being that sat beneath a dining table near the back of the room. The third being looked around before lowering its head to the floor and clasping its hands over its neck, while the second being turned to the table. The second being yelled at the third one, who ducked its head lower between its legs.

The first being in the armchair clenched its hands into fists while the creature above it began poking its sharp index finger into its ribs and leaned close to it. The creature in the armchair swung its clenched fist against the creature's jaw. The second being then backed up and covered its face with its hand.

The being in the chair curled up and turned its neck toward the back of the room where a staircase to the second floor could be seen. The being that was standing quietly sat on a couch next to the being in the chair. The being in the chair then looked at the one on the couch and went back to staring at the broken television.

Uri saw a shorter being tromp down the stairs, speaking its garbled language. More maroon slime oozed out of its pores. It snarled and emitted a screech.

The other three creatures quieted down as they turned to the fourth, who stepped forward. It appeared shorter than the others, about five foot eight, but it had the same pale flesh with visible veins along with a veil of maroon slime around its head.

It looked around at the other three beings. The first

being remained curled up in the chair, the second being stood with its head lowered, and the third stomped toward the window Uri looked through. She quickly ducked down and listened for a while. The walls vibrated as the creature stepped forward.

The four argued in a series of snarls and screams, each becoming louder and closer to Uri. Uri stuffed her communicator into her backpack and crept down the porch steps. As she stepped off the porch, she turned to see the doorknob turn. Uri dove off the porch and crawled to the side. She cautiously watched through the railing.

An impatient whine sounded from inside the house until the door swung open, smashing the window next to it. The shortest of the creatures stepped onto the porch and looked around. It scratched its ear roughly until maroon slime dripped down its hand. It stepped down from the porch and tromped toward the corrals.

Uri edged along the side of the house, watching as the being hopped into one of the corrals. The animals cried out as they ran around in terror. Feathers, flesh, hair, fur, and blood splattered onto the grass.

Uri looked back to the window and quickly lowered her head as the fourth being passed by it, emitting a mix of gurgling and snarling as it moved throughout the room. Uri listened as dishes and pots crashed to the floor. She looked into the window where the fourth being was blindly swinging its arms into the objects that occupied the shelves, pantry, refrigerator, and stovetop. It stopped and leaned over the countertop, its untrimmed nails scratching the surface each time it moved its fingers.

Uri heard the creature in the corral emitting its gurgling noise. She watched as it hopped back out of the corral, blood running down its fingers.

Uri crawled away from the window toward the back of the house. She froze as the third shorter being forced the door open and made clicking noises with its teeth. It then propped the back door against the exterior wall and dragged itself away from the farmhouse and toward the barn.

When Uri realized that the room was unoccupied, she quietly entered the house. She crept along the edges of the kitchen, avoiding the kitchen tools that littered the floor. As she was about to take another step, she saw a red and black leech like the one Liana had pulled out of her ear slowly crawling through the mess. It emitted noises similar to those of the four pale beings.

She crept along the rest of the clutter until she came to the dining room. A puddle of maroon slime covered the floor where the third being had been hiding. Uri knelt down and examined the slime. She looked up in time to see the third being stumble into the entryway of the dining room, its hand covering its face as though it had been punched. Uri ducked beneath the table and watched it stumble toward the fridge and take out a bag of frozen peas to place over its injury. As it lifted the bag to its eye, it looked toward the dining room. Uri could see deep into the being's empty gray eyes that peered through the maroon slime as it looked down.

The being gurgled and twitched as it took large steps toward Uri. The kitchen tools clattered loudly beneath its feet as it rushed to the table. It pulled the chair out from the table, threw it across the room, and ducked down to grab Uri. She turned away and pushed the chair out from beneath the table. The being screamed as the chair hit the floor, and Uri ran across the dining room floor and back into the living room. The noise of her running through the dishes caused the being to cover its ears and let out what sounded like the roar of a crowd. The being then slammed its fist against the floor, shattering the remaining dishes.

Uri ran out the back door. She could hear the clicking and screeching noises coming from inside the house. She hopped over one of the corral fences and ran through the mud, flesh, bone, and blood. She staggered up the hill behind the corrals and stepped into a dark green meadow laced with colorful flowers. "Please be here, Liana," Uri muttered as she began walking. Then she paused. She recalled that Liana's flesh matched the color of the grass. She looked down at the ground to keep from accidentally stepping on Liana and causing her to change her mind.

Uri crept around and called out, "Liana!" Her eyes shifted to the blades of grass rustling in the breeze. There was no tightly woven grass that formed the shape of Liana's body. "Did I get turned around?" Uri asked before calling out for Liana again.

A cold breeze flowed along the ground. It picked up leaves in small funnel shapes and carried them toward the edge of the forest. The grass shriveled into the dirt, clearing the trail that followed the leaves. "Liana!" Uri called out again. Her breath became visible as she hiked deeper into the woods.

A gust of cold wind overpowered the warm air from Liana's territory. The blue sky was taken over by gray clouds. Uri turned back to where the green forest ended. The smaller forest animals burrowed into their shelters, some hissing at Uri as she walked past them. The larger forest animals fled into the shadows as the air grew cold. Uri looked up to the sky. There were no snowflakes, only the small funnels of breezes cycling through the leaves. Uri wondered if the snow would fall soon. She hesitated and then turned on her communicator, only to receive a loud weather forecast: "Today's forecast..." Before the communicator finished, it automatically shut down. Uri tried turning it back on, but its screen remained off. "Please, do not let the world leaders call right now," Uri murmured. "I can't risk missing a call from them if my communicator is dead."

The cool breeze returned, carrying tiny red objects with it. Uri crossed her arms over her face as the objects caught onto the sleeves of her uniform. She knelt next to a tree trunk and rooted around in her backpack for a container so she could collect samples. The shards felt like pieces of plastic broken off costume jewelry. She dropped the shards into a plastic bag and proceeded up the hill. The hill grew rockier as Uri came closer to where two trees marked the top. She leaned against one of the trees for support as she hoisted

herself onto the top of the hill. She expected to feel rough-
ness as she ran her hand up and down the smooth bark and
examined the tree. The bark consisted of onyx with a fungus
made of diamonds scattered around its trunk. Her eyes followed the tree trunk up to the branches from which emerald leaves and rubies the size of apples hung. Across from
the onyx trees, a stream of aquamarine water carried pearls
at the edge of the land. Other onyx trees were adorned with
different colorful gems. A bridge of smoky quartz closed the
two-foot gap between the two sections of the gem forest.
On the other side of the stream sat a row of sapphire berry
bushes, with more emerald leaves, lining the path through
the gem forest.

Uri scooped up a handful of snow and watched it crumble into white pearls as it slipped between her fingers. As
she looked around at the beautiful gems, thoughts clouded
her mind. "This has to be the best place I've visited so far;
it's gorgeous," Uri said to herself. "Why hasn't Alondra or
Liana told me about this place?" Uri stopped to reconsider
what she said. "Why would they? They don't trust us humans enough to tell us anything."

Uri twitched when she was interrupted by a faint cursing
from something that sounded human. She looked around
for the Shadow and shuddered at the thought of finally
meeting it. "How would I speak to the Shadow?" Uri said.
She was unprepared for whatever the Shadow would be.
She had no weapons, only her communicator, which was
unable to pick up a signal. The only thing she could do with

her communicator was take pictures.

Uri tried to calm down by making up theories about the noise. "It's just another caretaker," she said. "Maybe Alondra has already told them about me." She wondered about that final possibility.

The Shadow appeared out of the corner of her eye, and she refrained from speaking. She tried to conjure up a better theory that it was merely one of the survivors. She breathed deeply and turned to the source of the cursing. Uri's eyes widened in surprise as she watched Kelvin Quick in the forest, turning around with a flashlight in one hand and furiously shaking his other in a fist at the sky.

"Kelvin?"

CHAPTER 14

Kelvin Quick spun around with a furious expression. He grumbled as he wiped the fog from his glasses. He smiled. "Hey, hey, Sergeant!" He embraced Uri in a hug and laughed. "What a pleasant surprise."

Uri pushed at Quick's chest as he tightened his one arm hug. Uri felt a large, heavy object hit her leg and looked down to see Quick still had his large briefcase, but it felt and looked like it contained something more expensive than the communicator he carried under his arm. "Kelvin," Uri gasped, "let go!"

Quick ignored Uri's request and continued his drawn-out hug.

Uri hesitantly lifted up her arms to return the hug before Quick pulled away and asked in an excited voice, "Hey! Are you looking to make a great offer on a great house?"

A look of confusion fell over Uri's face. She scratched her head as Quick looked at her with twinkling eyes. "Kelvin," she said, "what are you doing here?"

"What am I doing here, you ask?" Quick let out a faint laugh and his smile faded. "I'm in exile! Your wonderful Shamayim kicked me out when I was only trying to do my job!"

"What do you mean?" Uri asked.

"Before I happened upon your current predicament, I was selling houses for everyone!" Quick turned on his communicator to show a list of houses he had found.

"What exactly did you do to be exiled?" Uri asked as she swiped through the pictures of the houses. Uri bit her tongue when she realized that she could answer her own question by studying the pictures. As she continued through the listings, she saw that the houses would not meet the needs or expectations of the people on Shamayim. One house had holes the size of dinner plates along its exterior walls and roof; another house was missing all of its windows and its front door; and another house had been crushed, except for its front door, beneath the overgrowth of a nearby forest. Another house's doors and windows were blocked out with lumber and old signs reading "Condemned."

"Apparently," Quick snorted, "your happy little piece of heaven, Shamayim, doesn't like business. Well, I like business"—he beat his chest—"and if there is no business, I push! I go for it! I make a sale!" Quick finished his sentence furiously with saliva dripping from his mouth and a clenched fist aimed at the sky.

Uri raised her eyebrows.

Quick caught himself and returned to a professional state. He wiped the sweat from his forehead before calmly completing his story. "But of course, Shamayim couldn't handle me selling homes that are"—Quick cleared his throat before attempting to mock the voice of one of the Shamayim leaders—"'unsuitable for the modern family and at unreasonable prices,' so now I live in exile in the Wastelands."

Quick leaned over to look at his communicator's screen. Uri could feel Quick's tension build up as she flipped through image after image until she reached the final picture showing a log cabin with a broken sliding glass door as its only entrance. "None of these houses are suitable for anyone," Uri said. She even believed that she would agree with Shamayim's decision to exile Quick for his predatory business practices.

"Ha!" Quick said. "You obviously have no experience in the business of real estate, but I'm certain you'll find something soon."

Uri ignored Quick to study one of the listings. A rectangular red brick building stood with a sign that said "Memorial Hospital" in broken letters, and there was the Shadow with its face and hands pressed against a window next to the main entrance. "How did you get a picture of the Shadow?" Uri asked.

"Yeah, that abandoned house." Quick brushed the pearls out of his hair. "Make me an offer if you're interested; only problem is you'll need to look through the house yourself. I didn't want to get too involved in such a risky situation. I'm sure you understand."

"It's a hospital," Uri said.

"House, hospital, same thing." Quick shrugged. "I think you'll like it—lots of rooms, perfect for the adventurous type, if I know my clients well, and I should say I do." Uri flipped the image around.

"What about the Shadow? Were you able to speak to it?"

"Shadow?" Quick scratched his head. "The place was vacant, so let's talk about the price!"

"Do you not see the Shadow looking through the window?" Uri said, earnestly pointing at the image.

"Like I said," Quick insisted, "the place was vacant."

"First"—Uri held up the image to Quick—"tell me where you found this hospital and who lives there."

"I'm sure you can find it on your navigation—"

"Where's the damn building, Kelvin?"

Quick's smile tightened into a nervous grin as he threw up his hands. "Calm down." He then lowered his hands on Uri's shoulders. "I can show you the house...as long as you promise to buy it."

"No," Uri hissed.

"Very well." Quick shrugged. "I'll take my leave now." As Quick reached for his communicator, Uri pulled it away, and Quick fell face-first into the pearl snow. He lifted up his head, a scowl on his face.

Uri sighed. "If you walk me through the entire hosp... house," Uri said, "I will buy it." She watched as Quick's eyes lit up with a glimmer of hope. "But," Uri continued, "I need you to come with me after you show me the house."

The light in Quick's eyes died out. "You're not seriously planning to return me to that ridiculous city, are you?"

Uri leaned into Quick's face and growled, "I'm frustrated

by my current predicament, and it's only five foot five and wields a suitcase of clothing and a communicator."'

"Oh wow!" Quick gasped sarcastically as he stood up. "That is really rough."

"You're clueless," Uri muttered, and she passed the communicator back to Quick.

Quick shrugged and returned to his scrolling. Uri's eyes shifted to Quick's suitcase where she could still make out the odd bulges beneath the leather.

At least, I think that's clothing, she thought and sighed. "First, I wish to take a tour of the hospital."

"The house!" Quick corrected her.

"Right, the house." Uri rolled her eyes. "I would like a tour of the house." Uri watched as a goofy grin stretched across Quick's face. He grabbed her wrist and hiked through the piles of pearls.

"The house is not too far away," Quick exclaimed, "Trust me, Sergeant; you won't regret this decision!"

———⊜———

Uri managed to cut in front of Quick as he guided her through the gem forest. She figured that Quick would still try to sell her the hospital after returning him to Shamayim. Uri conjured up a price that sounded like something Quick would accept, and she turned her GPS on.

Don't think about that, Uri thought. *Just focus on your*

mission: locate and bring survivors to Shamayim.

"So...how much can you tell me about the hosp..." Uri began until she caught Quick's agitated glare. Uri let out a sigh. "How much can you tell me about the house?"

"Well," Quick said, smiling, "this house was one of the few that wasn't completely destroyed, I still find it strange that no one in Shamayim wanted it."

"Yeah, strange," Uri said mockingly. "I'm worried about you, Kelvin. You do realize you could be killed out here?" Uri watched as Quick turned his head with a displeased look.

"That's very possible," he said crossly. "But I've been through worse, and this house was not too terrible. You're just being quick to judge. Besides, did you even see where you were when we first met and I wanted to sell your house? That scrapyard was a nightmare. I don't know what I saw in your property."

"What you saw in my property?" Uri inhaled before she angrily said, "That's because I don't really have a choice about where I live; you do."

Quick scoffed and grabbed Uri by the wrist, taking his place in front of Uri again. "Well, since you're so insistent," he said, "I might as well let you have the house for free."

"No, Kelvin," Uri said. "Me returning you to Shamayim has nothing to do with real estate. You can't just wander around the Wastelands on your own."

"Say no more!" Quick said abruptly. "The house will be yours guaranteed."

Uri ignored the rest of what Quick was saying and tried

to contact the world leaders again in hopes of receiving another side to Quick's story. The screen turned on, and the words "Poor Connection" flashed across the screen before the communicator shut off again.

Uri looked up to see the Shadow leaping around in the distance of the gem forest. She bumped into Quick. "Ow," Uri grunted. She watched as Quick remained still. "Kelvin, what's the matter?" Uri asked.

Quick leaned forward as he looked down the path and scratched his head. Uri listened as Quick murmured, "Are we going the right way? Yeah, this is the right way."

"Are you sure you know where you're going?" Uri asked. She looked around at the different pathways scattered throughout the gem forest. Uri felt Quick continue to pull her deeper between two rows of ruby apple trees.

"Why wouldn't I?" Quick boasted. "I've hiked everywhere throughout this beautiful planet in search of the absolute best…"

Uri stopped, almost tripping over Quick's heels. She saw that Quick had knelt to the ground to look down the hill at the rest of the trail.

"Wait…was it this way?" Quick asked himself again while turning around at the other trails until he made a complete circle.

"Yeah, it was this way," he said.

Quick grunted as he pulled his suitcase closer to him. He lost his balance and stretched out his free hand to support himself against a tree. He panted and brought his hand over his mouth while looking around frantically.

"Do you need help with your suitcase?" Uri asked crudely.

"No, no, I can take care of myself!" Quick responded. He grabbed Uri's hand and sprinted through the pearls.

They passed by more rows of gem plants bearing larger cuts. Quick stopped, released Uri's hand, and gasped, "Sergeant, are you seeing this?"

"Why would this make you more excited?" Uri asked. "There were more gems back there."

"But, but, look at the size of these gems; think of their potential value."

Quick ran off to a tree covered in diamond icicles. Each icicle reached about five inches in length. Quick carefully twisted off one of the icicles and stared at how easily it slipped off the branch and into his hand.

"Wait! What about the hosp..." Uri paused and cringed as she reconsidered her words. "What about the house you wanted to show me?"

"The what?" Quick asked. His voice trailed off as he stripped a bush of its sapphire berries and emerald leaves.

"Never mind," Uri said.

She watched Quick wander deeper into the rows of onyx trees, plucking emerald leaves off of the branches. Uri turned to see the Shadow walking toward her. She looked back as Quick wandered deeper and deeper into the forest.

"I'll be here if you need anything!" Uri called out.

Quick shouted a brief "Okay!" and returned to collecting gems.

Uri held her head in her hand and murmured, "Oh God, I need to get him back to Shamayim before he gets himself killed."

Uri looked back to the forest. The Shadow was getting closer to her. Uri checked for any form of defense. "Wait," she said. "All of my stuff was destroyed in the theme park explosion." She watched the Shadow walk closer. Instead of a human figure, the Shadow's shape appeared more abstract as it pulled itself along by thick strands of fur.

CHAPTER 15

The Shadow grew more abstract as it walked toward Uri. Long streamers of black and blue hair waved in the breeze. They ran along the trunks of each tree and down to the ground. It then brushed its hair against the gems on the branches, being gentle so as not to knock any off.

Uri realized that this was not the same Shadow that had been following her. She studied the details of this creature and realized that this was possibly another caretaker.

The caretaker's black-and-blue hair extended toward Uri. She quickly lifted her hand to brush away the caretaker's tentacle-like hair and stopped as the strands flowed between her fingers. They were soft, similar to chinchilla fur, but they were long and thin like pieces of fabric. The caretaker then interlocked its other strands of hair with Uri's locks of curly black hair.

"Your hair is coarse like...," the caretaker said. His voice sounded like rocks rolling with the movement of the ocean.

Uri waited for the caretaker to finish but was surprised when he suddenly became quiet.

The caretaker looked back at the gem forest. His other

strands of hair extended to the nearby materials. He ran his hair up and down the onyx trees, through the pearl snow, and around the gems that made up the food in the forest. The hair wrapped around a smooth river stone and crushed it. The remains drifted onto the ground for the caretaker to examine. After running his hair across the material, he perked up.

"Sand," the caretaker finished his thought. "Your hair is like coarse sand."

Uri pulled at a piece of her black curly hair. She didn't realize how many months had passed since she began this mission in the Wastelands and that she hadn't taken the time to wash her hair.

She focused back on the caretaker, who now loomed over her in curiosity. His hair gently parted with the breeze revealing a large white orb in the center of his face, which Uri assumed was his eye.

"Your flesh too..." The caretaker paused, his orb turned to a light blue, and he scratched his head as if confused by Uri. "It's smooth, like a rock that has been long in the river." The caretaker scratched his head again. "But Alondra told me that you're a human."

More hair from the sides of the caretaker's body extended like two arms that wrapped around Uri and lifted her up to the orb in the center of his face. Uri struggled, trying to slip out of the caretaker's grasp. She stopped, recalling the possibility of her upsetting this caretaker after she upset Liana, and remained still as the caretaker finished his drawn-out examination of her.

"You are Sergeant Davida Uri, aren't you?" the caretaker asked in a deep, earthy voice. Gravel poured from his mouth as he spoke, and it landed on the ground sounding similar to large raindrops.

Uri inhaled the earth-scented fragrance lingering from his breath. The gray concrete-like skin of the caretaker poked through his hair.

"Yes," Uri said. She figured that Alondra probably had to describe her appearance in a way that this caretaker would understand.

"I am Damek, the caretaker of earth, and you're in time for the caretakers' monthly meeting," he said. "You know Alondra and Liana, correct?"

"I do," Uri said.

The white orb on Damek's face changed to a bright orange. Uri assumed that meant he would be more accepting like Alondra when she described her mission to her.

"Good," Damek said. "You are the exact human I've been looking for. You are required to join us at the caretakers' monthly meeting. In fact, I am traveling to the meeting place right now. It's only a twenty-minute walk from here; come."

Damek set Uri back on the ground and began walking to the left of the forest.

Uri turned back to the forest and found that Quick was completely out of her sight. She looked around and called out, "Kelvin! Where are you?"

Uri waited for a while.

"Kelvin!" Uri called out again. She grew nervous when Quick did not appear. Then Uri felt a tap on her shoulder and spun around to look up at Damek.

"This Kelvin, he is a friend of yours?" Damek asked. His voice was gravelly at first but grew smoother. "And you are a friend to Alondra and Liana, correct? Then Kelvin should be a friend of mine?"

"Yes," Uri said. She didn't trust Quick to be left alone, but she felt that Damek would have protested if she had suggested bringing Quick to the meeting. Alondra was the only caretaker who would take Uri's side in the matter of allowing humans into the Wastelands as well as communicating with them. Liana, however, didn't care about anything except the well-being of her plants. Depending on which caretaker Damek trusted more, Uri realized that she could possibly gain Damek's favor.

But that would be a fifty-fifty chance, she said to herself.

"Good, Kelvin can watch over the forest while we attend the meeting," Damek said with a nod. "Now come; the meeting is about to begin."

Damek slowly swayed as he plodded through two rows of gem trees, inspecting each of the fruits as he walked. His hair flowed along the different gem fruits, emitting a low hum as he navigated the forest.

Uri followed Damek, still searching for Quick's silhouette in the distance since she didn't see where he had wandered. She then looked up at Damek, who appeared not to have known about Quick in his gem forest until now. Uri grew concerned about how calm Damek behaved when he placed Quick in charge of the gem forest.

"Hopefully, Quick won't do anything to change Damek's mind about trusting me," Uri muttered to herself.

———— ≫《◉》≪ ————

Uri looked back every few steps to see if Quick was following her and Damek. She watched as Quick blended into the distance as she followed Damek farther from the gem forest. Uri felt one of Damek's appendages direct her face to his eye.

"As long as he does not touch any of the gems," Damek said sternly, "he should be fine."

"What happens if he touches the gems?" Uri asked, gawking at a tree covered in diamond icicles.

A deep growl rumbled from Damek's throat as he said, "You understand that these are all deadly for humans, correct?"

Uri knew nothing about gems other than whatever "diamonds" were advertised in Shamayim. She knew even less about Damek's gems. Before she could respond, Damek continued, "No human must ever touch these gems; they are strictly reserved for the sake of bringing nutrition to the planet for all of the new species to enjoy. These gems are poisonous to humans; therefore, they must never be touched or consumed by such a species."

Uri looked down at her hands as she recalled scooping up the pearls. Then she looked down at her shoes. "What if a human picked up a gem but put it back where it was?" she asked.

"I have yet to test that theory," Damek said. He leaned forward, and his orb turned green. "Why do you ask?"

"Just out of curiosity," Uri said, "but these are not actually gems. They're foods for the new species of Earth?"

"Correct," Damek replied. "We want to improve Earth by making a difference, not just by tidying up a measly wasteland. We restore everything that the humans ruined in each region. We bring peace to the world and defend it against those who would abuse it."

Uri cocked her head. "Who would abuse this peace that you bring to Earth?"

Damek shuddered as he said, "Those who would take the treasures of Earth for their own foolishness, their own greed, and their own needs. I, on the other hand, as well as the other caretakers, have chosen to remain wise to the powers of the new creations of the Earth. Therefore, we are the only ones capable of aiding in the restoration of Earth, not destroying it. Humans would only bring chaos back into our beautiful and newly reconstructed Earth."

Damek's orb turned to a neon green, and he stretched bunches of hair out to form a pair of arms. "Why would anyone risk the health benefits for money?"

"Money," Uri responded in a flat voice, "that's kind of

the only reason why anyone does anything."

Damek's orb turned orange, and his voice grew cheerful. "I must confess, Sergeant, you are possibly the wisest human I have ever met." He leaned over to look at Uri. "In fact, I believe that I will need to discuss the importance of your role in caring for Earth as one of the newly discovered caretakers."

Crap, me as a caretaker? Uri thought.

Uri reconsidered her meetings with the other caretakers. So far, Alondra liked her; however, Uri was the only human that Alondra had met. Liana was indecisive and refrained from comments directed at Uri. Liana chose to hibernate instead of providing an answer as to whether or not she would be willing to help humans. Uri decided to wait before asking for Damek's opinion on allowing humans into the caretakers' territories. "Damek," Uri asked, "why do you want me to be a caretaker?"

"You appear to be the only one qualified for the task," he said. "I doubt that anyone else would be able to perform your role; besides, Alondra recommended you."

"Have you or the other caretakers spoken with other humans?" Uri asked.

"We have no reason to," Damek said. "If we needed to speak to other humans, we wouldn't talk to you. Do you understand?"

"Y-yeah," Uri said. She looked around as the breeze rustled the onyx branches. "If you are in charge of the earth, why are you in a colder region?"

"We travel everywhere and have a variety of necessities that grow in different types of weather," Damek responded with a haughty laugh. "We exist to serve Earth and only Earth. You simply happened to locate me in a colder region while I was performing my tasks."

"I see." Uri nodded, trying to accept Damek's responses, even though his answers never provided a clear point. If anything, all of the caretakers, including Alondra, were avoiding the burden of answering Uri's questions.

"But what about the different territories? Wouldn't there be more caretakers? How would you readapt when crossing into a warmer or cooler climate? Or how would you even cross water? Do you have any obstacles like that?" she asked.

"We do not have 'obstacles.' We're all knowing and all powerful, and we have many other caretakers around the world," Damek huffed. "Humans are simply too ignorant to understand."

"Hold on." Uri stepped in front of Damek with her hand out, bringing Damek to a halt. "I get that humans have not accomplished what you and the other caretakers wanted us to accomplish."

Damek shook his head and walked around Uri. She sprinted around and stopped in front of Damek again. He let out another gravelly breath and gestured to Uri to let her finish speaking.

"However," Uri continued, sensing Damek's patience growing thinner by the second, "not all humans are evil—or ignorant, for that matter."

"What about your friend?"

"I'm keeping Quick on a short leash. I just need to look out for him until I can contact my leaders so they can take him back to Shamayim."

"They won't." Damek shook his head. "Do you humans only trust each other because you're the same species?"

"No, and what makes you think they won't take Quick back?" Uri asked.

"What about you?" Damek pointed. "I would assume they would want you back too if they want Quick back."

"I'm on a mission," Uri quickly responded.

"A mission?" Damek asked. "Alone?"

"Yes, I was sent out into the Wastelands on a solo mission to locate human survivors and return them to Shamayim, which is the city I come from."

"The Wastelands?" Damek scoffed. "Is that what they call our territories?"

"It's because we do not know much about what happened after the Mysterious War."

"War," Damek snapped. "What war?"

"The Mysterious War?" Uri said hesitantly. "Day by day everyone started acting strange, and no one knows the cause. People attacked other people, and no one could figure out what was going on, so they called for anyone still rational to travel to Shamayim."

Damek's orb turned a dark red. "There was no war. The caretakers would never start a war, much less start fights between each other; we're too peaceful; not only that, but your kind's situation resembles a pandemic rather than a war."

Uri tried gathering her thoughts but was only met with the typical chaos that clouded her mind. She was about to argue back until she saw Alondra and Liana walking toward her and Damek.

"Understand," Damek growled at Uri. "Only speak when spoken to, do not behave arrogantly, and accept all decisions as they are."

CHAPTER 16

"Sergeant Uri," Damek announced, "welcome to the Meeting Grounds."

Uri immediately recognized the Meeting Grounds as the same city the voices brought her to when they were inside her head. The only difference was that the city had none of the floating cubes.

Don't say anything about humans returning to the Wastelands and you won't be killed, Uri thought as she stood next to Alondra.

Alondra and Liana stood at the opposite end of the Meeting Grounds next to the other caretakers Uri had yet to meet. Each caretaker had a different swagger, voice, and visible aura that resembled the part of Earth they cared for. Uri chose not to introduce herself, as she already managed to upset two of the three caretakers she met. Instead, she quietly studied some of them.

Damek took an empty space between one caretaker who looked like sand caught up in a current of wind, which Uri assumed was either for wind or weather. Uri quietly took the open space next to Alondra. On her right side, a blue serpent-human hybrid rose out of a pool of water and

immediately engaged in a conversation with a large slug made of tiny insects.

Alondra entered the center of the circle and announced, "The annual Meeting of Caretakers has begun! We'll start with the water caretaker and rotate clockwise. Remember, you only have five minutes to announce your question or concern, and all other caretakers are not allowed to speak while the current speaker states their question or concern."

Uri hesitated regarding Damek's warning. She thought about the setup she used to try to persuade the first three caretakers she met to allow humans back into the Wastelands. Most of it was simplified information in an attempt to rush the process, summed up into a simple question: "what do you think about letting humans into the Wastelands?" This barely allowed Uri to persuade the caretakers. However, she considered allowing one human at a time to give the caretakers a better perspective of what they were like, starting with the world leaders.

Her thought was cut off when the water caretaker asked, "What do you think, Sergeant Uri?"

Uri's mind raced as she tried to catch up to what the caretakers were discussing. She could use this time to share about the world leaders. Quick also came to mind when she realized that Damek trusted him enough to leave him in the gem forest. Uri thought about the number of gems Quick already had collected after she and Damek left, and why Damek was so insistent about never touching the gems, and why they would be harmful for humans but not for the animals or the caretakers.

Then again, Uri thought back to how Alondra claimed that she wanted the humans' help in order to keep track of her animals. Uri hoped that if the other caretakers did not take her side, they would at least take Alondra's.

"Well, I guess it would be reasonable," Uri said before realizing that humans returning to Earth for the better possibly wasn't what the caretakers were hoping she would say.

"Reasonable?" Damek growled at Uri, "To let humans live on Earth? After all of the damage they've done?"

"Yes," Uri said.

Silence fell over the caretakers. Uri needed to keep them interested.

"Think about how much more would get done once humans were here?"

"We could use some extra help," Alondra said. "I'll admit that it has been difficult attempting to look after all of the animals of the Earth."

"'Difficult?'" Damek laughed. "We're caretakers; nothing is too difficult for us."

"Some of my animals have died," Alondra admitted. "I don't like the idea of humans living selfishly but—"

"You're kidding Alondra?" Damek said, cutting her off. His orb turned a blood red.

"I thought you wanted to restore Earth," Alondra snapped.

"Not the way humans wish to restore it," Damek said.

"Are you here to try to find suitable land only for your

species?" Liana hissed and pointed at Uri. "Typical humans."

"Survivors were located in the Wastelands," Uri said. "I'm just here to return them to Shamayim."

"Wastelands? Is that what your kind calls our territories?" the caretaker of wind said angrily.

"No! I'm trying to find this family, who is suspected of destroying Earth." Uri held up her communicator with the photos of the Shadow.

The caretakers exchanged glances. Alondra plucked Uri's communicator up and gently swiped through the photos with her hands. The other caretakers leaned in to examine the photos as well. Then Alondra said, "I feel like I've seen the Shadow before."

Damek growled, "You saw a monster destroying our territories and chose to do nothing about it?"

"I was waiting until our next caretaker meeting," Alondra said, her tone lowering to a growl.

"You're responsible for the animals, Alondra," the caretaker of wind said. "How could you let this shadow thing get out of control?"

"Uri," Liana hissed, directing the rest of the caretakers' attention back to Uri. "We want to help you, but we only care about the planet, not humans."

"If it helps…" Uri flinched when she heard her communicator announce one of the world leader's call. "I need to take this call."

She stepped away from the circle and answered her communicator only to be met with a loud and ecstatic world leader. "Sergeant Uri, I have great news! Turns out that Shamayim might have discovered some strange evidence off of the leech. Also don't worry about the bats; no one was harmed. It was strange how they just came and went. At least you are safe! Anyway, don't worry about giving LIES any details about where you are. I have your location mapped out on my communicator! See you in a couple of hours!"

CHAPTER 17

The ground shook as each caretaker unleashed a different wail. Some pointed to the sky while others shook their heads as they communicated through their agonized symphonies. The caretakers darted off toward their nearest territory location, leaving Uri behind. Uri looked at the dirt road and trails twisting throughout the city. Each trail was lightly coated with a certain material unique to each territory. Uri followed the path covered in patches of fur and feathers from Alondra.

Uri ran through the mess. She tried to contact a world leader again. Unfortunately, her communicator continued to shut off after displaying a screen reading "Poor Connection."

She pulled up her navigation on her communicator, and the application immediately closed out, indicating that she wouldn't be able to connect with Shamayim again. She began to sweat, her mind still on the return of the world leaders.

Uri couldn't think of a reason for the caretakers to not allow humans into the Wastelands. She flinched as a realization hit her. "What am I thinking? Humans are so idiotic; even I would agree with the caretakers that we do not belong on Earth."

She looked at Alondra's path. Tiny versions of the prism lizard crawled along the buildings, fading in and out with their movement. Other animals from Alondra's rain forest gathered at the edge of the path to devour the fresher parts of dying plants. As Uri continued along the path, the animals backed away as if they understood about the deadly power their caretaker possessed and how it would be used if Uri chose to anger Alondra.

"But there has to be some reason for all of these new creatures," she muttered. "However, how much of said explanation will only make Shamayim keep me here even longer?"

Uri thought back to Quick. Despite Damek's warnings, Quick still decided to try to steal from his forest.

Uri flinched when she heard a roar in the distance from one of the caretakers. "Why am I thinking about Quick now? I need to think about the danger the world leaders are in!"

She tried to call the world leaders' office for the third time. The screen read "Poor connection" again and then "Warning: Dead battery; plug in your device to recharge" before completely shutting off. Uri tossed her communicator into a nearby swamp and started walking in the opposite direction of the way her communicator originally wanted her to go before it died.

Uri pressed her fingers to her temples as her thoughts collided. She could barely comprehend what she was trying to accomplish. "Crap." She spat when she realized that she had completely strayed away from the trail that Alondra took. "Now I wish that I tried to fix that communicator."

Her thoughts directed her down a couple of paths, which still had patches of fur and feathers, that led into a dense rainforest. The first trail brought her to a water hole where different animals were lined up in the shadows. After one glance Uri turned back on the trail. The second trail guided her to an area where tree branches bound together blocked out sunlight and provided the forest with a tunnel-like appearance. Uri decided to try this path, despite an intense impulse to want to find a different one.

She caught a glimpse of the eyes of a large feline and several canine-like creatures glaring at her from the overgrowth. She looked down and saw that she was knee-deep in the water. "I need to be more careful," she told herself as she stepped farther into the tunnel, "otherwise World Leader Jordan is really going to get on my case."

Uri could barely imagine what she would tell World Leader Jordan about the leech, the caretakers, and the fight for Earth. It was such a collision of events that built up and tore down potential evidence for locating survivors at the same time. The caretakers would need to be willing to communicate with humans, and the humans would need to learn not to try to take over. Uri predicted that both sides would not sacrifice power.

"I cannot be on both sides," Uri muttered as she imagined the chaos that would ensue once that happened. She looked up and noticed that she was close to the end of the tunnel. At the edge of the tunnel was a patch of sunlight resting over an algae-laced pond.

"Think of the positive outcome, and stop overthinking the situation, Davida," Uri scolded herself, "and stop thinking about which side will possibly surrender Earth."

A voice from outside of the tunnel called out, "Who is surrendering Earth?"

Uri stopped and stepped into the opening of the tunnel and gasped at who was waiting for her at the end, "Oh fu…"

Márquez stood at the end of the tunnel. He was damp with a mix of rain and sewer water. He smirked as he examined Uri before responding, "Well, hello, Sergeant."

Uri watched Márquez's lips move; however, her eyes were fixed on the rips in the shoulders of his uniform. She tried to focus on Márquez again but couldn't help but look at the cold glares from the different swamp animals in the shadows.

As the two exited the tunnel, Uri massaged her temples before responding. "Why are you here in this rainforest, Márquez?" Uri asked.

Márquez cracked his neck into place and said coldly, "Weren't you listening? I'm here to search for my student who was picked up by those large bats."

"Who?" Uri twitched. She reconsidered asking if Márquez had returned to the academy already. However, it was obvious that he was completely out of the academy's range.

Uri watched as Márquez turned up a steep hill that

covered the tunnel. She followed along toward a moist jungle similar to Alondra's territory.

"Héctor Chávez," Márquez hissed. "The student you spoke to when you 'happened upon' the academy."

Uri responded with a blank stare. It wasn't until she recalled Chávez's dark-brown eyes in the shadows of the rain forest that she completely remembered the entire event. She wondered if Márquez was still upset about the intrusion of LIES yet refrained from asking.

Uri collected her thoughts again, realizing that she had kept Márquez waiting too long for her response. "Yeah, the academy that is meant to be a secret, but all of its buildings are skyscrapers in the middle of a rain forest." Uri rolled her eyes. "Do you ever wonder how I found your school?"

Uri stopped herself when Márquez leaned in centimeters away from her face.

"Yes," Márquez hissed, "that one. Now, if you don't mind, I would like to finish my explanation."

Uri twitched, and she motioned for Márquez to finish.

"Chávez was also picked up by the bats and I was sent out to look for him once the bats left," Márquez said, "the academy also suspects that there are more missing students."

"Why not send out a search and rescue team?" Uri asked.

"You do not work for the academy; therefore, I refuse to tell you anything other than I'm missing a student, and after months of searching, I'll finally admit that I need help. But I only need help with looking, not returning to the academy or sending Héctor to attend a second graduation ceremony, which must now be held because someone attracted a bunch of monstrous bats."

Uri muttered, "Fair enough," and she hiked onto a hill stitched together by tree roots. "Are you familiar with a family by the name of Hawkins?"

"No," Márquez said. "Who are they?"

"A family who is possibly responsible for the Mysterious War."

"You mean the pandemic, right?" Márquez cocked his head.

"That's right, and I want to see if my mission to locate survivors has anything to do with the Hawkins family."

"Wait," Márquez said and pressed his fingers to his temples, "who are the survivors?"

Uri provided a brief explanation of her mission, why the Shamayim government appeared at the academy, and who the caretakers were, as well as the leeches and their connection to the Shadow that followed Uri.

Márquez stared at Uri with a puzzled expression on his face. "Let me get this straight," he said and scratched his head. "On your way to finding survivors and the academy, I guess, you are stalked by this Shadow and have been guided by a leech that lived inside of your head but was removed by a what?"

"A caretaker," Uri said. "A being that devotes their life to caring for Earth. However, everything they create ends up dying anyway. Not only that, but this new species of parasites that look like leeches have been created."

"Hold on," Márquez sighed. "So, all of this is a result of some group, cult, or whatever taking over the world with these leeches and doing what exactly?"

"I don't know."

"And these caretakers and other strange creatures are somehow alive as a result of all of this?"

"That's very possible. I spoke to one, and she said that the caretakers just existed one day."

"They simply came into existence? No explanation? No creator?" Márquez said. "Not only that, but what do the caretakers look like? Are they animal-like? Plant-like? Mineral-like?"

"Well," Uri hesitated, "yes."

"Well, that makes everything easier," Márquez snapped.

Uri attempted to briefly cover her history with the caretakers for Márquez, why they lived on Earth, and why they supposedly hated humans. Unfortunately, she ended up throwing out excruciatingly long stories, including every inch of detail about the places she'd traveled to, including the sightings of the Shadow that followed her. Her words continuously rolled off of her tongue.

Uri believed that she would finally convince Márquez of the existence of the caretakers as well as the Hawkinses and their possible connections with all of these newly discovered species.

"Do you expect me to believe you?" Márquez cut Uri off.

"Sure, those large bats could have been an undiscovered species, but the three beings you described couldn't possibly exist due to the fact that you've been in isolation for as long as you have. Besides, do you even have a clue as to who these Hawkins people are?" Before Uri could defend herself, Márquez continued down his long list of explanations for Uri's stories. "Come on now," Márquez laughed, "you could not have possibly traveled as far as you did, as you would have had to grow weak. There is no help outside of Shamayim and the academy, as we know how to survive and gather our own resources."

"Those necessities were provided by the caretakers and whatever supplies I could find. I basically did the same things as you."

Uri's words ran together as she ducked beneath a web of vines. She believed that Márquez had grown bored with her answers due to how quiet he became. *I wonder if I could conjure up a more interesting response*, she thought.

"If you speak to one of the caretakers," Uri added, "you shall receive all the answers."

Uri watched Márquez tilt his head up and let out an impatient sigh. Márquez's voice lowered as he asked his next question. "Are you some type of trickster? Do you do this for fun?"

"No," Uri said firmly as she bit back her anger. "Why can't you just trust me?"

"The entire academy still holds you accountable for

the bat incident, no doubt. Even I won't believe your story about these caretakers until you provide me with evidence."

Uri looked around in frustration. She caught the flashes of scales from the tiny prism lizards scurrying between the trees. One of them eyed Uri and skittered up a tree, emitting a hissing sound.

"Great, now I need to find more of those colorful birds and, hopefully, Alondra," Uri muttered to herself. "Shouldn't ten- to twenty-foot-long bats be enough to convince you of what the world has come to?"

"Alright," Márquez hissed, "let's try this again."

Uri focused on finding Alondra while Márquez spoke. She wandered down a trail and found it covered with more patches of fur, similar to when Alondra left the Meeting Grounds. Uri only picked up fragments of what Mr. Márquez said.

"Let's say we do find these caretakers." Márquez brushed a curious family of rainbow quail away from his feet. "What happens next?"

Uri felt uncertainty course through her body. She could only imagine what the caretakers would do to Márquez once he was introduced to them. Uri barely knew anything about their powers other than their "abilities" to clean up the mess left behind by humans.

"We'll try to have them help us find your student," Uri said.

"You're just going to talk it out with eight-foot-tall

monsters who hate humans?" Márquez gasped. "You're insane!"

"I get that you hate the idea, Márquez." Uri tried to respond calmly. Unfortunately, anxiety overtook her voice. "But at least try to run with it."

"I do not run with sheer stupidity," Márquez huffed. "You'll need to try harder to convince me about these human-hating entities and how they will aid us in finding Chávez."

Uri paused for a while in an attempt to understand Márquez's words. Eventually, she called out, "Alondra!"

"Quit shouting," Márquez whispered as he covered Uri's mouth. "I don't want to d...Oh my God."

Uri felt Márquez's hands slip away from her mouth, and she watched him drop to his knees and point toward a shadowy section of the forest. The trees swayed followed by the sound of heavy footsteps. Birds burst out of the treetops squawking complaints. Uri peered into the shadows to see Alondra's ivory skull slowly emerge.

"Oh," Uri exclaimed, "there's Alondra."

She looked down at Márquez who now crawled toward an overgrown path. As he tried to squeeze through the entrance of the narrow path, Uri reached out and pulled Márquez back by his shirt collar.

"What do you think you're doing?" Uri scolded Márquez. "The caretakers are here to help us. Try to stay on their good side."

Uri could barely make out Márquez's small whimpers and turned back to Alondra, who was now kneeling in front of them. Alondra leaned her head toward Márquez who continued to stare at her in fright.

"Do not gawk," Uri whispered to Márquez before she turned to Alondra.

"Alondra, I can explain," Uri began. She stopped when Alondra held up her hand.

"Sergeant," Alondra grunted, "the caretakers grow restless; even I'm struggling to believe you when you say you will help us figure out who destroyed Earth."

"Can't we return to the Meeting Grounds and sort all of this out?" Uri asked.

"Do you realize what we're possibly up against?" Alondra snarled as she sat on her hind legs and stretched out her arms. "Intruders!"

"Can we please just hold another meeting about all of this?" Uri asked again.

Alondra relaxed her posture. She turned her head to face Márquez and Uri.

"Please let Márquez live," Uri barked. "Now, how long will it take everyone to return to the Meeting Grounds?"

"I'll see what I can do," Alondra said. "You'll return to the Meeting Grounds, and I'll try to convince the other caretakers to join us, but I cannot guarantee that the outcome of our next meeting will tilt in your favor."

Alondra guided Uri and Márquez along. Uri saw Márquez

trying to climb through the space between the trees, and she pulled him back and brought him to her face.

"Would you cut that out?" Uri whispered to Márquez and slapped him. "You're being very rude."

After receiving no response, Uri pulled Márquez along. "Honestly, I thought the academy trained you to be better than this."

Uri felt Márquez twitch as he said, "So did I."

CHAPTER 18

Márquez slapped Uri's hand away from his shoulder and followed her and Alondra at a distance of five feet. Alondra looked back and lowered her head to Márquez.

Uri detected hints of disapproval in Alondra's walk. She then turned to Uri and growled, "Make sure he doesn't cause any problems."

Uri nodded as she thought back to the caretakers' meeting. Each caretaker possessed some ability to understand their own territories yet lacked the knowledge of the needs of their fellow caretakers' territories, as well as how humans could help.

"Alondra," Uri asked, "will the other caretakers agree to at least try to speak with my leaders?"

Alondra hesitated. "It's possible, since we already have humans here." She pointed to Márquez. "Not only that, but us caretakers keep running into issues that make it difficult for us to perform our duties. I truly stand by the humans, that is, if they are willing to help as you claim."

Uri glanced back and saw Márquez captivated by a group of multicolor frogs crawling along on the thin tree branches.

Seven of the different-colored frogs lined up in the order of a rainbow and croaked in different sounds similar to a drum set. Uri rushed over to pull Márquez away as more frogs continued to line up along the other branches.

Uri sighed and turned to Alondra who gestured at Márquez in disappointment. "I fail to see how this one could help us," she said.

"Right now, he's looking for his student, Chávez," Uri replied. "Afterward, he'll return to the academy where he works."

"What about these world leaders?" Alondra asked. "How do they plan to aid us?"

"The world leaders should be able to provide a full explanation of this situation regarding the survivors," Uri responded quickly.

"I see," Alondra said.

Uri sensed the doubt in Alondra's voice. *I need to maintain Alondra's trust*, Uri thought.

Uri looked up as Alondra plucked a piece of fruit that resembled a misshapen pomegranate out of a nearby tree and snapped it in half. She placed one half in the trees for the birds and gave the other half to Uri.

"Once I meet these world leaders," Alondra asked, "what will they say?"

"The world leaders will want a meeting similar to the caretakers' meetings," Uri said as she split the fruit in half again and passed the second piece to Márquez.

Uri looked back to make sure Márquez was eating the fruit. Instead he turned the fruit around in his hand and sniffed at it before nibbling a piece.

"How would the humans help us caretakers, exactly?" Alondra asked.

"We may know why you're struggling to maintain control over the new life of the Earth," Uri said.

"Is that so?" Alondra perked up. She allowed a neon bluebird to land in the palm of her hand. Alondra began plucking ticks out of the bird's feathers.

Uri watched in surprise as the bird let out tweets of pain. Once Alondra finished removing the ticks, the bird flew out of her palm. Alondra tossed the ticks into the bushes and continued checking the other birds for the same issue.

"I thought you bred every animal to be vegetarian?" Uri asked.

Alondra's back grew tense. She lashed out at Uri, "I did!"

"Then why did this bird have ticks?" Uri asked.

"Remember what I said?" Alondra lowered her voice. "It's not easy for me to keep up with every creature. That's why I need help from your kind, Sergeant Uri."

Uri turned to see Márquez run toward her, and Alondra turned away to tend to a family of three-eyed deer resting in the shadows.

Márquez pulled Uri behind one of the trees and watched Alondra briefly look over her shoulder before turning back to tend to the deer.

"What was that about?" Márquez whispered to Uri.

Uri looked over to Alondra, who was grooming each animal's strands of fur for similar problems with the bird's ticks.

Uri shrugged and followed Alondra again.

"Wait," Márquez tugged on Uri's shoulder.

Uri followed Márquez off Alondra's path and onto a different path covered with moss and fallen trees. Márquez watched until Alondra moved on to care for other animals.

"Look, Sergeant," Márquez said in a panic. "I don't know if this is some kind of prank, but it's very convincing."

Uri gestured to herself and asked, "Does it look like I would be able to create Alondra for the sake of a prank?"

Uri and Márquez turned back to see Alondra coax another neon bluebird onto her index finger.

"You obviously have powerful beings on your side," Márquez said as he nodded nervously to Alondra. "To be frank, I'm walking in circles trying to find my student by myself."

Uri looked back to Alondra. She realized that Alondra was staring back at the two of them with her empty eye sockets directed at Márquez. Uri quickly looked back to Márquez and allowed him to finish.

"I will need..." Márquez bit his tongue in the middle of his sentence. "I will need someone else to help me find my student, Héctor Chávez," he said.

Uri raised her eyebrows. "You need help?"

Márquez rolled his eyes before he continued. "I would like us to split up so we can cover more ground while we search for my student."

Uri gave Márquez a questionable stare. She then looked

back to Alondra and the animals moving in and out of the forest.

"Why me?" she responded. "Why not someone from the academy?"

"I can't get anyone else from the academy to help," Márquez snapped. "They all chickened out after the bat incident."

Márquez clinched his hands and lowered his head, "Wait," he said. "Let's say you do find my student; then how will you find me? We have no means of communication."

"What if I return you to the academy, and then I'll go find Chávez?" Uri asked.

"Screw that!" Márquez snapped. "If you don't remember, the last time you showed up at our academy a swarm of bats attacked us!"

"I thought the bats left you unharmed," Uri said, as she narrowed her eyes.

"Well, they did," Márquez said, "but they took my student as well as a couple of other students and staff members."

"I see," Uri sneered. "But at this point, you're either lying because you're scared of Alondra, after I told you to not be rude to her or the other caretakers, or you do not want to take refuge in Shamayim."

Márquez shook his head. "Fine, but I don't like the idea of letting the caretakers help us."

Uri tilted her head. She looked at Alondra, who was now glancing at them while caring for one of the smaller variants of the prism lizard.

Uri took that as a sign that they needed to continue toward the Meeting Grounds.

"Very well," Uri responded, "I'll find your student."

<hr />

Uri and Márquez walked back to Alondra. Alondra finished disposing of the ticks from a neon bluebird and moved on to three frail jaguars who eagerly circled a patch of grass. Uri crouched down and made out a round object in the center of the jaguars. She crawled closer to see the shape of a turtle tucked away in its shell. The largest jaguar gnawed at the turtle's shell until it could break off a piece. Another jaguar snarled, and the other two looked toward Alondra. Alondra let out a roar like a lion, and the three jaguars fled. Uri and Márquez looked at each other when they heard Alondra mutter strange curses as she knelt next to the turtle. Uri crept up to Alondra's side to see that the turtle's shell had been broken into pieces and chunks of its flesh were eaten.

"Alondra?" Uri said. She felt Alondra's fury about the turtle's demise grow more intense as she whipped her head around and responded with an annoyed, "Yes, Sergeant Uri?"

Uri stepped back from Alondra before asking, "What about the meeting?"

"Forget the meeting!" Alondra barked. She raised her head to the sky and yelled, "All of my animals are killing each other! The caretakers' territories are failing!" Alondra looked back to Uri, and her voice let out a raspy cry. "How could you think of a meeting at a time like this?" Alondra then turned to Márquez and growled, "You."

Uri watched Márquez shrink back as Alondra extended a sharp finger at him and said, "I don't know what you are up to, but something tells me you're in on the destruction of Earth."

"What?" Márquez exclaimed. "No!"

Alondra pressed her forehead to Uri's, "You're in charge of Márquez!" she shouted. "How did he manage to wipe out half of my animals?"

Márquez pushed Uri away and got in Alondra's face. "I had nothing to do with your animals dying." He pointed at Uri. "And Uri is not in charge of me."

Alondra looked back to Uri. Her head twitched, making the aligning of her spine more audible. "Then who is in charge of Márquez?"

"My employers," Márquez cut in, "but right now my employers need me to look for my student."

Alondra turned away from Márquez only to find that the turtle had died during her rant. Alondra scooped up the turtle's remains in her hands and went to the tree where the three jaguars had escaped. The jaguars glanced at each other and gave Alondra gestures of innocence as she approached the tree. Alondra started pointing and holding the turtle's remains up to the jaguars while shouting about the "destruction they were bringing to Earth." A smaller jaguar leaped out of the tree branches and snatched up the turtle's remains in its mouth. It crept back into the shadows, ignoring Alondra's demands for it to return. Alondra shouted, "I took care of you!" to the jaguars and glared at them as if she was waiting for an apology. The jaguar with the turtle in its mouth looked down and spat up saliva and chunks of the turtle's remains into Alondra's right eye socket. As the jaguars fled from the tree, Alondra rubbed the edge of her socket, loosening a piece of meat that got caught on the edge of the bone. "They stopped listening," she grumbled before shouting, "Continue, Sergeant Uri!"

Uri felt a chill cycle through her body as Márquez stared nervously at her. "First, I would like Márquez to finish his explanation," she said.

Alondra took a breath and made a humming noise as if she were counting. She moved on to tend to another neon bluebird that was infested with ticks and exhaled harshly. "Go on."

Márquez ran his words together as he replied, "I need to find my student. He might come into contact with a family known as the Hawkins. Do you know them?"

Alondra thought for a while. "Ah, yes. Damek warned me about the good-for-nothing Hawkins family. They believe in destroying the beauty that we were meant to restore."

"Well"—Márquez shrugged—"can you help me find my student, as well as the Hawkinses?"

"I will," Alondra said. "Lucky for you, I care about humans as well, since I'm not completely ignorant like Liana and don't hold grudges like Damek. I will help you with all of your needs."

Alondra and Márquez exchanged glances. Alondra then turned to Uri and asked, "What do you propose we do, Sergeant Uri?"

Uri closed her eyes. She caught a single faint whisper travelling from one of her ears to the other. She scratched inside her ear and looked at her finger to see that it was clean of the maroon slime. She rolled her tongue against the inside of her cheek. She felt a small bump along the side of her mouth, but it was so tiny that it felt more like a taste bud than a leech.

Uri looked back to Alondra and Márquez, who were still waiting for an answer. Her words rolled off her tongue with ease as she said, "We need to host another caretakers' meeting."

CHAPTER 19

Alondra wandered through Damek's territory. Over one-third of the trees had been stripped of their onyx bark down to their quartz sapwood. Alondra looked down in order to step over the broken gems scattered along the ground. She ran toward a tree that bore pear-shaped emeralds. She plucked off one of the emeralds and bit into the gem. She gagged and spat out the chewed-up gem. She then moved on to a tree with peach-shaped moonstones. She pulled off one of the moonstones, took a bite, and spat it out before barely tasting it.

Uri looked over to Márquez. He was in the same hypnotic state that Quick was in when she and Damek left for the caretakers' meeting. Márquez scooped up the white pearls from the ground and allowed them to run through the spaces between his fingers.

"Hey," Uri said, shaking Márquez from his hypnotic state. Márquez shot Uri an agitated expression, and Uri calmly replied, "Do not take any gems from this forest."

"What happens if you take them?" Márquez asked as he slowly reached out to touch a raw diamond icicle attached to an onyx branch.

Uri swatted Márquez's hand away and walked around a jade hedge to try to avoid any backlash she would receive. Uri realized that she never received a direct answer from Damek about the gems and had nothing to combat Márquez's actions. She looked back at Alondra, who now ran her fingers along the branches to feel and collect samples of the jadeite leaves.

"They're simply not meant for humans," Uri responded.

Uri flinched as Márquez's eyes narrowed. She watched timorously as Márquez stormed up to Alondra and cleared his throat.

"Alondra," Márquez began.

Alondra looked down and let out a low growl from the back of her throat. "Yes, Márquez?"

"Why are you doing this?" he asked. "Why would you try to take our world away from us?"

"Your world?" Alondra laughed. "You humans were in charge of your world and look at the mess you made! We do not want to take your world away. We caretakers simply want to aid you in the reconstruction after this Mysterious War you humans find fascinating."

"Mysterious War?" Márquez asked. "What's that?"

Uri turned Márquez to face her. "I'll explain. For a while, humans behaved unusually, and it increased into a large group."

"Sounds more like an epidemic than a war," Márquez said.

Alondra looked around at the other fruit trees. She

snarled and growled as she took bites of the fruits. "Damek, your fruits are flavorless!" Alondra shouted as she stormed through the forest.

Márquez leaned toward Uri and whispered, "Who is Damek?"

Uri looked around. She remembered leaving Quick behind to attend the caretakers' meeting and wondered why Damek trusted him. However, she couldn't remember where Quick ended up in the forest. Her thoughts were interrupted when Alondra chose to call out to Damek again.

"How do you expect the caretakers and my animals to eat?" Alondra looked around before raising her voice even louder. "Which, I would like to add, are all dying, thanks to you!"

Alondra looked around as the wind picked up. The pearls on the ground shifted as Damek approached them.

Uri studied Damek's appearance. This time he was hunched over, and his eye looked dim compared to when she first met him. His long blue and black hair wrapped around the damaged forest as he dragged along a strange object covered in red minerals. Damek dropped the object, revealing Quick's corpse covered in clusters of the mineral cinnabar.

"Alondra," Damek whispered, "I trusted this human"—he gestured to Quick—"and I was wrong to do so."

Alondra knelt down to examine Quick's corpse. She broke off a chunk of the mineral and sniffed it before looking at Damek and snarling, "Is this going to be the result of allowing humans on Earth again?"

Uri and Márquez watched as Alondra lunged for Damek. Damek lifted his arm up in defense as Alondra pushed her forehead against Damek's and let out a low growl between her teeth. Alondra's words changed to the snarl of a wolf at first but quickly reverted back to Uri and Márquez's language.

"Well, you were wrong to trust that man without consulting Sergeant first!" Alondra wailed.

Damek punched Alondra's jaw and yelled, "You treat Sergeant like she is a caretaker!"

Alondra realigned her jaw and pushed Damek back while shouting, "Sergeant is a caretaker!" Alondra spat saliva and blood onto Damek's fur.

"Is that so?" Damek yelled. Gravel spilled from his mouth, speckling the pearl snow. "If Sergeant is a true caretaker, why did she not look after this human?" He pointed to Quick.

Alondra let out a hissing sound similar to a snake being threatened. Her hand latched onto Damek's throat and shoved him into a tree. The onyx bark shattered, and Alondra laughed. "Did you really expect these onyx trees to hold up? Onyx is fragile! You should have known that!"

Damek pushed Alondra onto the blanket of pearls on the ground, yelling something that came across as a curse to Uri.

Uri stepped back, pulling Márquez with her.

"You're just going to walk away?" Márquez panicked.

"Can't you stop them?"

Uri ignored Márquez and stared off in the distance to see that the Shadow still followed her. The Shadow jumped back and forth over a gap between two small cliffs, appearing oblivious to the fight occurring about a yard away. It leaped to a ruby tree and plucked off a handful of rubies and diamond icicles.

Uri couldn't believe it when she saw that the Shadow appeared completely unaffected by the gems. She shook Márquez to make him focus on the Shadow as well.

"Who is that?" Márquez spat.

"I don't know"—Uri took a deep scared breath—"but it has followed me ever since I began my mission."

Uri watched as the Shadow gathered sapphires from the bushes. It paused and looked in their direction.

"Damek?" Uri asked. She saw that Alondra and Damek were still fighting, completely oblivious to the Shadow stealing from the gem forest.

Uri turned to Márquez. His face was a mix of awe and fright as he too studied the Shadow.

"Where did you first see it?" Márquez asked.

"At an amusement park next to my old base," Uri whispered. "However, it ended up destroying both the amusement park and my base."

The Shadow faced them after it broke off a piece of an onyx branch.

Alondra and Damek's heads jerked toward the Shadow, who looked back at them and dragged the onyx limb with all of its strength.

Alondra unleashed a loud shriek similar to a human scream, causing the Shadow to jump back and trip over the uneven ground. It landed in a bush of emeralds, gathering as many of the broken shards as possible before it crawled away.

Damek held out strands of his hair, causing pearls to heap onto the fleeing shadow.

The Shadow plucked the pearls off of its body and shoved them into Quick's suitcase. It got up and ran deeper into the forest. Uri looked over at Márquez who watched in surprise as the Shadow made its escape.

"That person has been stalking you this whole time?" Márquez asked as his eyes followed the Shadow while it danced toward the shadows.

"Yes." Uri quivered. She turned her head when Damek screamed.

Damek pulled his hand away from his face, revealing a large chunk missing after Alondra scratched it. Damek wiped off the blood, jumped onto Alondra, and grabbed her head, forcing it into an onyx tree trunk.

"Have you tried killing it?" Márquez whispered as he watched the Shadow strip another bush of its sapphire out of Alondra and Damek's sights.

"It's too fast," Uri answered as she watched the Shadow perform its balletlike movements around the forest. "Once I get it in my sight, it disappears. This is the first time it has allowed me to look at it for this long."

Márquez carefully looked over the Shadow as it twirled around a ruby apple tree. It stood on its toes and cautiously studied each ruby before picking it and stuffing it inside Quick's suitcase, managing to be swift enough to dodge Alondra and Damek.

The Shadow stopped and looked toward Uri and Márquez. Uri couldn't make out its facial features as it remained in the shadows. The Shadow quickly pulled off a handful of emerald leaves from the bushes and sprinted deeper into the gem forest.

"Alondra? Damek?" Uri looked at them in time to see blood trickle down Alondra's fingertips.

Damek backed up, running strands of his fur along the fresh wound Alondra had left on his cheek. He pulled his fur away to watch as dark red magma blood dripped onto the pearls.

Damek retaliated by shoving his hands into Alondra's mouth. Blood trickled off his arms as he pushed past Alondra's fangs in an attempt to pry her jaw off of its skull.

"Would you two stop?" Uri yelled. "The Shadow is getting away!"

Alondra and Damek stopped to watch the Shadow make its escape. Damek picked up Alondra by the neck. "Do you see what you did?" Damek shouted. "You're too easily distracted and allowed some thief to escape with my gems!"

"Oh please," Alondra barked, "you can make more!"

"While your animals starve!" Damek boomed as he leaned into Alondra. "Do you realize how long it takes for my gems to grow so I can harvest them?" He tore off a ruby apple from a branch and held it up to Alondra. "Do you know how many years it took me to grow this apple tree? Do you think I'm going to let all of this hard work go to waste for a couple of measly humans who wouldn't have even thought to rely on other materials for food rather than animals?"

Alondra grabbed Damek by the back of his head and shoved his face into the pearl snow. Alondra hissed, "Define 'years.' I know you're a slacker." Alondra lowered her head next to Damek's ear. "Your fruits are either unripe or rotten by the time I get them, and my animals end up either starving to death or eating their own kind because of your lack of production."

Uri jumped in between the two caretakers with her arms spread out. "Will you two cut it out? The Shadow got away!"

"You heard the new caretaker, Alondra." Damek coughed up blood and snickered, causing the pearl snow to kick up. "Why don't you listen to her like the rest of the caretakers?"

Alondra groaned and whipped around to glare directly at Uri. Then she turned to smack the back of Damek's head. "Very well," Alondra hissed. "What do you propose we do about our current predicament, Sergeant?"

Uri thought for a while. She recalled that Alondra refused to attend the next caretakers' meeting due to the tragic event involving animals reverting back to their carnivorous ways. She wondered if Damek's poor gardening skills were the result of Alondra's destructive animals or simply the fact that animals wouldn't be able to live off plants alone.

"What about Liana?" she asked. "Doesn't she grow plants for food?"

"Plants that allow oxygen to flow!" Damek corrected Uri. "Liana's plants are poisonous to anyone who eats them." He leaned into Alondra. "You of all caretakers should know that."

"Liana's plants are not poisonous!" Alondra argued. "I happen to feed edible plants to my animals every day!"

Damek grabbed Alondra's neck, causing her joints to crack. "That should tell you a lot! Why don't you blame one of the other caretakers for once?"

"That's enough!" Uri shouted.

Both caretakers looked down at Uri. Damek released his grip from Alondra's neck. "So, Sergeant Uri," Damek groaned, causing the ground to shake for a couple of seconds, "continue with your proposal."

"We still need to find Chávez, and I'm supposed to locate survivors."

"Damek," said Uri. She turned and Damek groaned as he listened, "Once we find these survivors, we will return to Shamayim and leave you and the other caretakers alone. That is all I am doing."

Damek returned to a relaxed stance. He brushed his hair out of his eye to look over the path that the Shadow had taken. He exhaled a deep breath and responded, "Very well, we shall return to Liana."

CHAPTER 20

Alondra and Damek stormed along in silence. Damek appeared to hold the larger grudge of the two as he carelessly shoved passed the onyx trees, causing gems to fall and shatter on the ground. Animals that were prey quietly crept out into the open, attempting to scrape together whatever fruits they could before they were surrounded by predators. Uri looked up to Alondra, who turned away as a feral dog barked at a three-eyed gray wolf. The dog's threat ended rapidly as the wolf pounced on it, followed by a flurry of the dog's blood.

Uri watched as the pearl snow gradually led back to the asphalt road littered with abandoned vehicles. Alondra followed the direction the vehicles were facing, cautiously stepping over broken glass and mutilated corpses. Uri studied the shattered glass next to a few of the cars. Fresh blood dripped from the edges of some of the windows, and Uri realized that someone else had recently traveled through this place.

Could it be survivors or the Hawkinses? Uri thought.

Uri looked over her shoulder as Márquez hovered over a faded black luxury car and ran his fingers over the rusty exterior before diving into the bashed-in front window of the car. Uri grabbed Márquez's shirt collar and pulled him out. She saw that Márquez had a couple of wallets encrusted in dry blood clutched in his hands. Uri slapped the wallets out of Márquez's hands and dragged him back to the caretakers.

Uri caught up to Alondra and Damek, who were chattering. She eased closer so she could hear them.

"What will we do about this Hawkins family?" Alondra asked Damek.

"I say we wipe out everyone and everything"—Damek clinched his fist and held it to the sky— "including Uri and Márquez's territories, since humans are useless to us. Afterward we'll start from scratch and create our own species and territories."

"Do we know if the Hawkinses are human or other caretakers?" Alondra asked, looking over her shoulder at Uri. "Or some other species for that matter?"

Fear pulsed through Uri as she backed away. She tried to remain within earshot as the caretakers continued their conversation.

"Who cares?" Damek responded. "Even if they were caretakers, I doubt they would be willing to help us restore Earth."

Uri's mind raced as Damek spoke. She wondered how much of the truth she would be able to give Liana before Alondra and Damek pushed their beliefs on her.

"Besides," Damek continued, "what difference would it make?"

"What do you mean?" Alondra grunted.

"We'll just find other ways to design new species. We do not need humans on Earth as much as we simply need replacements."

"Replacements?" Alondra hissed. "Are your ears clogged? We are not replacing the humans."

"Then what will we do with the humans?" Damek pointed back to Uri and Márquez.

"We'll make them help us restore Earth," Alondra responded.

Uri jumped back and whispered to Márquez, "Jaime, are you picking up on any of this?"

"You've already said that," Damek huffed as Uri and Márquez continued to eavesdrop. "The other caretakers know that none of the humans except for Sergeant Davida Uri, is willing to help us restore Earth."

"Here's an idea," Alondra squawked. "Since Sergeant Uri understands the function of a human being, we'll place her in a domain over the humans."

"Sergeant Uri claimed she isn't a caretaker for the humans." Damek gritted his teeth.

"Hear me out, Damek," Alondra pleaded. "We'll find some way to convince the humans to help us care for Earth."

"How?" Damek grumbled.

"We'll grant the humans freedom in exchange for their work," Alondra suggested in a prudent voice.

"What if they refuse your offer?"

"Well," Alondra hesitated.

Uri watched as Alondra grew tense while she tried answering Damek. Damek eventually lost interest and wandered off to a patch of dirt on the side of the road to give it nutrients. Alondra grew furious and stormed over to Damek. She snatched him up by the longer strands of his fur and turned him around until their faces were inches away from each other.

"If they refuse, we can kill them," Alondra finished with a hint of poison in her voice.

"I thought you were against that idea," Damek responded as he scooped up a handful of dirt and held it up to his eye. "You wanted humans alive to help us restore Earth." Damek paused to think about her response. "Although, I can see that you have taken my ideas into consideration."

"It's still wrong to cause a massacre for the sake of restoring Earth." Alondra lowered her head. "Besides, who knows what wonders bringing in another species would do to Earth."

Uri drowned out the rest of the caretakers' conversation as it grew distorted. Eventually, the caretakers resorted to arguing in their traditional language. Uri at least relaxed when the caretakers did not resort to physical fighting this time.

Uri groaned as she recalled how, unbeknownst to her, she was deemed a caretaker while struggling to convince survivors to trek to Shamayim. At the same time, she was constantly stalked by some strange shadow that remained in the shadows and performed seemingly innocent gestures.

Uri looked out of the corner of her eye. She barely made out the Shadow leaning over the handlebars of a motorcycle while staring at her from a distance. She quickly looked away and looked back only to see it had disappeared.

"Now I'll be kicking myself for not making Márquez and the caretakers look at the shadow." Uri cringed.

The group reached the edge of the abandoned vehicles that led to what, as Uri recalled, was Liana's territory.

She looked up to see the Shadow standing fifteen feet away on the side of the road. The Shadow looked back and proceeded to run around the vehicles, busting windows with its bare fists as if it was punching through Styrofoam. The shadow's hands dropped to its sides, and streams of blood dripped onto the ground. The Shadow looked down for a while to admire its blood dripping onto the asphalt.

Alondra and Damek exchanged glances and whispered to each other.

"Will the Shadow follow us?" Márquez asked Uri.

Márquez's question flew over Uri's head as she stared at the Shadow.

The Shadow shook the blood off of its hand before slowly lifting its head up to look at the group. It tilted its head to the side as if it were deciding whether or not the group was a threat.

Uri exchanged glances with the group and the Shadow. The Shadow then ran onto the side of the road and toward the forest where Liana's meadow began. The group looked toward the off-ramp and ran toward the entrance of Liana's meadow.

"Alondra, is that one of your creations?" Uri asked.

"No," Alondra said. Her voice trembled.

The Shadow ran away from the group and deeper into the meadow.

"Quickly!" Alondra shouted. "The Shadow must be stopped."

Alondra and Damek chased after the Shadow, and Uri and Márquez followed.

Uri believed that Liana wanted to get away from the chaos the caretakers enforced as a whole. Liana even showed signs of weariness as she ran off to find the world leaders.

Alondra pushed her way through the trees until she reached a meadow of dead grass.

Liana sat in the center of the meadow with her arms wrapped around her knees and her chin resting on the tips of her thumbs. Her skin was pale gray as opposed to her usual green hue.

Uri, Márquez, Alondra, and Damek all leaned over Liana, watching for any signs of life.

Liana rubbed her eyes as she regained her rich green complexion. She pulled her hands away, revealing brownish daisies surrounded by violet circles around her eyelids. She slowly rose to her feet while looking around at the group.

Alondra and Damek crowded closer to Liana and asked if she needed help, what attacked her, and if the attacker was still near the meadow.

"Can you tell us anything, Liana?" Alondra gently placed her hand on Liana's shoulder.

"Don't touch Liana." Damek smacked Alondra's hand away. "Your hands are bony and cold!"

"Liana." Damek reached out to her, his strands of fur gently wrapped around her hand. "What do you need?"

Liana smacked Damek's strands of fur away and she plodded through her meadow, wearily uprooting the dead plants and weeds in her path. Uri watched in horror as Liana hunched over, almost in pain.

Liana muttered to herself while violently uprooting a bunch of stinging nettle. She threw the nettles down and hissed in pain. Red bumps formed on her hands, and she let out a scratchy cough before she continued weeding. She scratched at her flesh, causing the bumps to darken and ooze aloe vera.

"Those vile Hawkinses," Liana spat. Her voice grew raspy with each word she spoke. "They think they can set foot wherever they want; they think they can just appear and ruin my plants!" Liana roared and turned to face everyone. "One of them appeared. I mistook him for one of Alondra's deer; however, this Hawkins thing came in and destroyed my meadow!"

"Can you tell me what this Hawkins family member looked like?" Uri asked.

Liana huffed as she said, "This one; why I couldn't kill him is beyond my comprehension, but like I said, I thought he was one of Alondra's animals. Before I knew it, I watched him tear up the grass and flowers in my meadow and flee as I chased after him. After he left, I became ill from the sight of my desolate meadow and fell asleep for a long period of time."

Uri ran her fingers through her now thick, curly hair. While in the Wastelands, she realized the she only managed to find one survivor, Márquez, and had no way to reach Shamayim after her communicator died. She looked over to Márquez. Uri considered trying to take him back to the academy. That way the survivors would be easy for the Shamayim government to locate since they'd already journeyed there.

"What about my student, Héctor, and the academy where I work?" Márquez cut in. "I have yet to hear a straight answer from any of you regarding my student."

"Márquez," Uri said, "we will find your student and return both of you to the academy."

Alondra leaned over Márquez, completely ignoring Uri's reply. "A caretaker is recovering from a brutal fight," she snarled, "and you're worried about your student, who could still possibly be alive?" Alondra then grunted, "That is, if your student didn't decide to adopt your attitude and get himself killed."

Alondra turned back to Liana, who was speaking abruptly to Damek, pointing to the plants and then to the soil.

To Uri, it appeared as though Liana was blaming Damek for providing poor soil for her plants. Uri could only shake her head. Alondra motioned for her to follow her away from the others. Uri walked away followed by Márquez.

"Where are you going?" Márquez hissed.

Alondra turned to Márquez and pressed her index finger to her teeth before she pointed toward the woods. Uri followed Alondra's finger to where the Shadow ran between the trees.

"Oh my God," Márquez said. "Sergeant, why are you following this thing? I thought it was trying to kill you."

"I never said that," Uri replied, "but I need to know if it is a survivor."

The Shadow continued motioning for Uri to follow it. Uri slipped through the trees and started following the Shadow. She felt Márquez hold her back by her arm.

"Where do you think you're going?" Márquez hissed.

"Maybe the Shadow knows where your student is," Uri answered. "Remember, I promised I would help you find your student."

Uri received a blank stare from Márquez. "I want to find my student and return him safely to the academy," he said, "not get killed in the process."

Uri then looked back to see that the Shadow appeared to be waiting for them, still motioning for them to follow it.

"Besides"—Uri looked over to see that Alondra returned to talk with Liana and Damek, who were still arguing about the Shadow—"the caretakers have yet to resolve any of their problems."

Uri and Márquez cautiously followed the Shadow. The Shadow responded by looking back and pointing to where it planned to go before taking off in that direction.

"Do you think the Shadow will also know where your survivors are located?" Márquez asked. "Or if it will be willing to cooperate with us?"

"It's possible," Uri said.

She looked back to see the caretakers locked in an argument. They appeared to no longer care that the Shadow was still in the forest. She then looked back to the Shadow. Whenever the Shadow stopped, it waited until Uri was a few feet away before running to the next tree.

Uri finally caught up to the Shadow. She looked up into its gray eyes as it leaned forward revealing a pale-skinned male face. Blue veins pushed against the underside of the Shadow's flesh. Its lips curled back revealing its lightly maroon-stained teeth.

Uri could only think that this was the thing that followed her during her entire journey. She remembered the Shadow's actions involving the destruction of Earth's landmarks; the theme park, her base, and the city crowded Uri's mind.

CHAPTER 21

An intimidating grin stretched across the man's face as he shoved Márquez aside and rapidly approached Uri. The man leaned into Uri's face, stepped back to circle her, and repeated his actions. Uri felt as if the forest was expanding, creating gaps between the trees. By now, she was convinced that she still had remnants from the leech left in her brain. Uri also did not doubt that this was from her processing the fear rushing through her mind. She quickly assumed this man only wanted to intimidate her, and she decided to remain expressionless and wait for the man to speak.

Unfortunately, the man resorted to stranger actions. At first, he backed into the shadows, causing Uri and Márquez to turn around in response to every faint sound in the forest. He then silently appeared from behind another tree and continued to circle Uri and Márquez.

Uri looked back to see that the caretakers were still caught up in their argument, resorting to snarls and groans.

"Alondra!" Uri shouted. Alondra did not hear her.

"Hey, Alondra!" Márquez tried. Alondra did not hear him either. The three caretakers remained trapped in their argument that they still called a "meeting."

Uri's body grew cold the more she lost track of the caretakers and continued to follow this man. Uri saw that Márquez only looked at the man in fear. She gave Márquez a look that said, *Why aren't you fighting? Do you even know how?*

Márquez appeared to have forgotten that Uri was there and only focused on the man. She wondered what was cycling through Márquez's mind as the man circled them again.

Uri thought, *I could pry information out of this man*. She decided to start with the primary question: "who the hell are you?"

At first, the man was surprised by Uri's rudely stated question; however, he quickly responded in a polite manner that made Uri and Márquez equally uncomfortable.

"You do not need to be afraid," the man said, holding up his hands in defense. "I understand that you are searching for survivors, so allow me to help you."

Uri and Márquez exchanged glances. Meanwhile, Uri also considered the many times she had lost evidence for her commanders due to this man's actions. A deep groan sounded from the back of her throat as she demanded the man's name.

"I want your name first," Uri hissed.

The man's smile stretched even wider. "Why?" he asked in a sly voice. "Don't you only refer to me as 'the Shadow'?"

Uri felt fear and impatience cloud her mind as she

rephrased his question. "What are you?"

"I am Benjamin Hawkins, and I am exactly like you."

Uri and Márquez looked at each other and then back at Benjamin.

Benjamin rolled his eyes and let out a faint laugh. "What did you expect me to say? That I'm an alien? Or a demon? Or whatever you believe in?"

Benjamin's voice trailed off as he crept behind Uri and Márquez.

Uri watched as Márquez flinched and muttered, "crap," when Benjamin wrapped his arms around their shoulders.

"I'm willing to make peace with your kind," Benjamin offered in an oddly kind voice.

Uri shook her head. "No, you've destroyed the caretakers' territories and convinced them that all humans were to blame for the destruction of Earth"—Uri's fiery eyes met Benjamin's somewhat surprised expression—"which would explain why almost all of Earth looks like a desolate wasteland."

Benjamin snickered, "What we've done has improved the earth."

"Everyone is on a wild goose chase to save their own skin," Uri hissed. "You've simply caused a massive epidemic in order to force everyone to believe that they were in danger, and now I'm stuck searching for these chickens that were too scared to find shelter on their own."

Uri pointed to Márquez as she scolded Benjamin.

Benjamin gently shook his head and laughed. "You

obviously are under some type of control." He reached out and opened Uri's eyelids even wider. Uri responded by swatting his arm away.

"Maybe it's from the toxic fumes; maybe it's from that junkyard you lived in." Benjamin's eyes narrowed to Márquez. "Maybe it's from isolation and the fact that you could never prove yourself."

Benjamin walked away. Uri felt a cold tension in the air as Benjamin headed toward a clearing in the forest. There, a wall of concrete wrapped around and connected in a circle.

Uri and Márquez followed Benjamin to a five-foot hole in the wall with only a few passersby who had physical characteristics similar to Benjamin's. The citizens passing by glared at Uri and Márquez as they stepped through the hole.

Uri made out the shapes of unfinished construction sites and a few human silhouettes hiding behind dimly lit windows. All looked similar to Benjamin. Everyone watched with disturbing glares that gave Uri and Márquez a hint of what would become of them if they failed to communicate with this new species.

Uri pressed her fingers to her left temple. Some of the citizens made low chattering noises among themselves as they watched Uri and Márquez follow Benjamin through the city. Uri tried not to stare at any of them, yet her eyes wandered as the citizens appeared to glare at her. Uri quickly turned her head to the side and saw that some of the citizens in the distance resembled Benjamin while Uri only knew him as the Shadow.

The citizens' unsettling glares pierced Uri and Márquez. Márquez leaned over to Uri and growled, "Well, are these the survivors you've been going on about?"

"Are they, Sergeant Uri?" Benjamin turned around and continued walking.

Uri perked up as she listened to the leeches whisper to her, "These aren't the survivors."

Uri scratched the inside of her ear. She pulled her hand away to see orchid-colored slime drip down her finger. Uri thought back to the leech that Liana removed from that same ear. "Did it reproduce? How long have I had other leeches since Liana removed the first one? Did I see the slime on it when Liana removed it?" Uri asked herself. She guessed that the vision of her in the apartment was due to the leech.

"What is that?" Márquez said as the slime traveled down Uri's hand, leaving a purple stain on her flesh.

Before Uri could respond, her body was shoved forward. She dug the toes of her boots into the dirt to keep from falling. She and Márquez looked back to see a citizen quietly step back into the crowd that had lined up near the side where Uri walked. The citizen scowled, followed by a roar of laughter from the citizens.

Márquez bolted through the crowd, and the citizen ran through the crowd as well, attempting to escape from Márquez. However, Márquez rapidly caught up to the citizen who pushed them and raised his hand to smack him. Uri reacted by reaching out to grab Márquez's hair and pulling both of his arms behind his back, while Márquez struggled to attack the citizen. As Uri pushed through the crowd with Márquez, some of the citizens cheered for Uri, but a few booed in hopes of starting the fight again.

Uri looked back, and her eyes met the citizen's glare. The citizen spat up a strange liquid that did not resemble blood, saliva, or vomit. Instead, it appeared to be similar to the goo from her ear in both texture and color.

Márquez slowly refrained from attempting to attack, and Uri released him from her grip.

Whispers filled Uri's brain as she pushed the palm of her hand against the side of her head. She felt a long, slim creature squirm beneath her skin. Uri hoped that the leech would starve and become intensely thin to the point that it would leave her in search of a new host. However, she was unsure about what the leech was feeding on or how it survived.

She scratched her ear again as she felt the leech pull itself into two, with the new leech crawling in the opposite direction of the first one.

The first leech then whispered to Uri, "Look to your right."

Uri's eyes flickered as she looked to her side where one of the citizens grasped his head tightly and pushed it against the side of the wall. She watched as the man rammed a different part of his body into the wall of a building, as if attempting to relieve his pain. A woman approached the man and knelt to the ground to pick up something. Uri watched as the woman raised her hand, and she quickly looked away to avoid the sight that was to come. However, the sight on the other side was no better. A cluster of citizens surrounded a woman who was lying on the ground. Two of the civilians gathered at each of the woman's limbs and began pulling in opposite directions.

"Oh, we failed to realize that that sight was on the other side," the leeches snickered in response to the citizen being pulled apart.

Uri shook her head to throw the voices off as she prepared to enter what Benjamin called Glass City's Main Government Building. Inside, the lobby was a simple dark blue color with picture frames and well-polished wooden furniture lit by florescent lamps with smooth silk shades. Benjamin slammed the door behind them, startling Uri and Márquez, but he also appeared to do it to maintain their attention. He began introducing Glass City and its history by claiming that they were a species "sent by unknown forces to cure humankind," similar to the report Uri received when she was first sent on her mission. The rest of Benjamin's words faded as the voices continue to draw Uri's attention.

Márquez leaned over to Uri. "Why do you keep looking around like that?"

Uri caught her head twitching in different directions and realized that the voices had gained some possession over her body again and were forcing her to look around. "I can't really explain that," Uri whispered.

Márquez rolled his eyes and changed the subject. "What

will you tell this Hawkins family? Will you be able to convince them to restore the academy and return the survivors?"

Uri grew quiet as Márquez's words repeated in her brain. She never came up with a solid plan for gathering survivors, and currently Márquez was the only survivor she located. Uri also recalled that Márquez still held his search for Chávez over her head.

"Remember?" the voices hummed. "We said we would give you the words to speak whenever you approach members of authority." The voices then laughed and continued, "We might even help Márquez find Chávez if he wants."

Uri blinked as the furniture morphed into abstract shapes before turning into a different style. The polished desk became a busted desk, and the lampshade turned into an old cloth one with worn edges. The walls also changed to a grotesque white with visible dirt and smoke stains.

Benjamin's pale flesh turned a sickening green. Uri doubted that it had anything to do with the lighting.

"We have some survivors who might be willing to go with you as well." Benjamin tapped his fingers against the desk as he spoke with a strange happiness in his voice. "The group will also have your student."

"No!" Márquez barked. "I only came for my student, and I'm leaving with only my student!"

"I'm sure you will." Benjamin took an agitated breath that turned into a yawn. "However, there's a catch."

Benjamin firmly grasped Uri and Márquez's shoulders and turned them toward a door at the end of the building's entryway. Uri felt the leeches squeal in agony in response to the short, sharp scraping noise Benjamin's teeth made as he ground them together.

"So, Sergeant Uri," Benjamin began as he pushed Uri and Márquez forward to make them keep walking, "if you want to free the survivors, here is what you will need to do." He rolled his head around in thought and said, "You need to give us something in exchange." Benjamin looked up to the ceiling and smirked.

Uri and Márquez looked up at the ceiling as well and then responded by glancing at each other. The ceiling was covered in thousands of leeches similar to those inside Uri's ear. The leeches squirmed around creating whispers and laughed in response to what was said. Some of the leeches left behind the same orchid slime, giving the ceiling a glossy appearance.

The leeches wiggled to the ground as quickly as possible, nibbling at the walls on their way down while Benjamin continued speaking.

"You apparently have some method for surviving Earth's Wastelands and possessing those caretakers, so we want you to stay with us in exchange for letting the survivors return to Shamayim. You will be very useful to us."

Uri and Márquez waited for Benjamin to provide some explanation for his request, as well as for why the leeches squirmed closer to them. Instead, Uri and Márquez watched as Benjamin knelt down and stretched his arm out to allow some of the leeches to slither up. He rose back to his feet, still showing some thought about his request.

"Also," Benjamin smirked, "I think you should keep whatever number of leeches are slithering around inside of your head."

"Are you kidding me?" Uri ran her finger along the inside of her ear. "How or why do they keep returning to me?"

"They help us maintain our citizens better"—Benjamin shrugged—"so they should help you while you work beside us."

"Wait." Márquez scratched his head. "Did you create these abominations?"

"Not us." Benjamin shook his head. "That one maned wolf thing who calls herself a caretaker did, only I think she originally intended the leeches to be harmless."

Benjamin listened to the sound of a crowd of people getting into a fight rise from behind the doors. "We just stole the leech because we like to see how many riots we can start with a single tiny creature that someone created and took pride in."

Uri watched as the leeches slipped into the cracks in the walls and floor. They slithered outside the building, and an even louder uproar sounded from the citizens.

"You're just now realizing that?" Benjamin scoffed. "It's a method common in the Hawkins family, as well as any other humans in general."

The fights outside slowly came to a halt as the leeches left the citizens' ears and crawled back inside the Hawkins family's building.

Benjamin turned away and continued, "These survivors

are possibly the only creatures that can be presented to your leaders; however, they may not be well received."

"May not?" Uri hissed. "Shamayim is so safety oriented that your citizens wouldn't make it past the first entrance!"

Uri watched Márquez lean closer to the window, and she followed his actions. Outside, a group of citizens sat below the window. A few of the leeches squirmed out from the cracks in the building and lodged themselves in the citizens' ears. The citizens began screaming and gripping their heads before they started beating themselves.

"You, Sergeant Davida Uri," Benjamin said, "appear to be the only one who can get along with the leeches. Everyone else tends to fight them. Oddly enough I find myself resisting their voice as well."

"You chose to do absolutely nothing about the leeches?" Uri couldn't imagine why the citizens of Glass City would be open to listening to them. "The leeches lie to and confuse everyone. Why would you allow that for your citizens?"

"Don't ask me." Benjamin held up the palms of his hands in defense. "Either ask some other member of the Hawkins family or one of the villagers. I'm certain they will be happy to talk to you."

Uri looked down as a leech wrapped itself around her leg. She reached down and gripped the leech's entire body. She pulled it off and twitched as the leech shrieked. Its squeal sounded closer to gasping as it squirmed in her hand. Uri dropped the leech, and it slinked back into the shadows. She looked down and saw a purple stain smeared across the palm of her hand. Uri rubbed at the stain, but it did not come off. She licked the stain as well, yet it refused to even smudge.

"Ignore them." Benjamin waved his hand and forcefully guided Uri and Márquez down a hallway aligned with single wooden doors. As the three proceeded down the hall, Uri looked around. The single wooden doors changed to large iron prison-cell doors.

CHAPTER 22

enjamin walked toward the back of the building where everything was completely quiet. Uri imagined it was a prison; however, she expected a collection of howls rather than one. Empty cell doors lined the walls, giving the howl a more eerie feel. Uri saw that Márquez seemed more confused than afraid and that Benjamin remained unfazed by the howls. Uri wondered if the howls were from the leeches.

"Stop!" Benjamin's voice boomed. "You're here."

Uri and Márquez were turned to face a pair of iron doors that led to a hallway lined with steel prison doors. The first prison door contained a small hunched-over boy. He didn't flinch or speak as Benjamin opened the door and shoved Uri and Márquez inside.

Uri and Márquez looked at each other and then back at the boy.

"Hey, you." Uri leaned against the cell door, tightly gripping the cell's bars in her hands.

The boy looked up in response, revealing a pair of dark brown eyes.

Uri recognized those eyes from the shadows of the rain

forest—the eyes that had stared at her through an electric fence. They were the eyes of Márquez's student, Chávez.

"Oh my God!" The leeches gasped in response to seeing Chávez. "And you didn't believe us when we told you we would guide you to survivors."

The leeches let out roars of laughter and slithered around Uri's head. Some of them threw themselves against the side of her skull. Uri pushed her fingers against her temples in response to the pain while attempting to listen to Benjamin.

"Here is your student, Márquez." Benjamin pointed at Chávez and turned back to the open cell door. "Now leave us."

Uri and Márquez exchanged glances. Even the leeches ended their whispering, surprised at Benjamin's demand for Márquez and Chávez to leave Glass City.

"Wait." Márquez stared at Benjamin. "Why are you releasing us?"

"I'm releasing you and your student, since you're both completely useless to me." Benjamin pointed to Uri. "However, I still need Sergeant Uri."

Uri tilted her head as the leeches protested, their voices spewing gibberish. The leeches then grew silent when Uri asked Benjamin, "Why do you need me?"

"You're currently the only one who can successfully work alongside the leeches," he said.

The leeches slammed into Uri's frontal lobe. She groaned and held her head in her hand. "I say you blow up this godforsaken city as soon as Benjamin turns his back on you," one leech boomed. The rest of the leeches collectively agreed and chanted, "Destroy Glass City! Kill everyone! Including the survivors!"

Uri rolled her head as she thought about her next response. Instead her thoughts shifted back to communicating with the leeches. "You do understand that I don't have any weapons left, I have no one I can contact, and I have a group of people that I still need to rescue, right?"

"That's true," one leech whispered, "so let us do all the dirty work."

Uri twitched at the leech's response. She looked at a nearby wall mirror and saw her black irises shift to gray. The room faded to a gray scale, save for Márquez, Chávez, and Benjamin.

Uri focused back on Benjamin when he snapped his fingers to draw her attention to him.

"Well, Uri," Benjamin began in his false friendly tone, "I want to know why you're the only one who can control the leeches in your head. No one else in Glass City can do what you do."

"Huh? Why is he only giving you credit? What about us?" the leeches asked.

Uri gently rocked her head from side to side. She searched for an answer as the leeches squirmed around her brain. "I don't know," Uri responded. "We're kind of stuck together for now. We've simply managed to maintain a decent relationship."

Benjamin appeared surprised by Uri's response. "Have you tried removing the leeches—surgeries, flushes, anything?" he asked.

"Not me, but a caretaker did." Uri thought for a while. "However, I assume that the leeches managed to reproduce before the removal and kept themselves well hidden."

"Where would this caretaker be now?"

Uri shrugged. "Anywhere by now."

Benjamin sighed, "It's a good thing Glass City is prepared for anything."

Uri listened as the leeches began chattering again. They sounded tense and agitated. She watched as Benjamin grew tense as well, possibly due to the leeches occupying his head.

Benjamin circled Uri, still refusing to believe anything she said. "I still can't see how you can live like that, voices constantly going all day, every day, and the voices never grow weary. You always remain strong and resist the urge to kill and destroy anything in your surroundings."

Uri wondered the same thing. Her eyes focused on Benjamin as more of the maroon slime trickled from her ear canal.

"Maybe I could lead you to the caretaker of the animals," Uri suggested. "It's not very far from here."

Benjamin sighed impatiently. "Glass City does not wish to communicate with humans who are attempting to keep these leeches under control."

Uri watched as Benjamin twitched and massaged his

temples. Agony crossed his face as a wormlike bump slithered beneath his skin. "The leeches are meant to keep us under control," he hissed. "We're not meant to control the leeches."

A blank expression crossed Uri's face. The leeches squirmed across her brain again, each one muttering, "How will you respond to that?"

"I don't understand," Uri replied flatly. "You say you want to help control the leeches, but you also say that it's impossible to do so."

"It is impossible to control the leeches!" Benjamin barked. "Yet you've managed to do it yourself, and since you apparently refuse to listen to me, I need to explain every little detail to you again."

The leeches snickered in response to Benjamin. "Maybe we should introduce him to Alondra. I'm sure she'll be happy to help." The leeches finished their sentence collectively in a grim tone.

Benjamin proceeded to explain his need for Uri again in a harsh voice. Outside, a group of civilians cried out, different from when Uri first entered Glass City. Benjamin looked out the window, muttering, "Don't mind the civilians; they're fighting again."

A glass bottle crashed through a nearby window. More screams poured into the room, followed by the sound of citizens scurrying around the perimeter of the building.

"Those screams do not sound like protests," Uri murmured. She looked out the broken window and studied the mass of civilians as they gathered at the base of the building. One civilian at the front of the crowd screamed incoherent words, and the crowd charged the building and pounded their fists against the doors. Uri held back the vomit that pooled in her stomach as wood splinters dug into the civilians' skin and blood trickled from their hands.

Uri looked up at the source of the civilians' actions. In the distance she saw the tall wolflike silhouette of Alondra ambling toward the building.

Some of the civilians turned to Alondra and cried when the building's doors remained shut. The civilians scurried to move out of Alondra's path as they pursued the building, despite Alondra's nonaggressive actions. Groups of civilians shoved past Uri and Márquez as they climbed through the window. Glass cut their flesh, sending more agonized screams throughout the building.

Uri pushed through the crowd, attempting to reach the broken window. A civilian grabbed Uri by the back of her jacket and threw her out of the window. Uri stretched out her hands to brace her fall. Her flesh hit the sharp edges of the glass, and she hissed. Uri jumped out of the window and onto the ground where she continued to fight the chaotic crowd.

"You call everything I said to Benjamin 'the words to speak'?" Uri screamed at the leeches as she pushed citizens out of her path. "And this is the result?"

"Hey!" the leeches snapped. "Alondra's here! What more do you want?"

"I still need to make sure that none of the survivors get killed!" Uri snapped back.

Uri twitched and kept her eyes on Alondra. The citizens and objects in her peripheral view morphed into the peaceful city Uri envisioned when she first came to Glass City. The cans and bottles transformed into pieces of paper being scooped up and tossed around by the wind.

"Would you cut that out?" Uri hissed at the leeches. "Changing what I see doesn't make anything better!"

"Fine!" an alto voice sang.

Uri's sights shifted back to an aluminum can barreling toward her face. The leeches forcefully tilted Uri's body to her side as the can brushed by the shaggy curls of her hair. The leeches forced her to walk forward in a calm manner as the riots continued. Slowly, the leeches forced Uri's mind to think again about the peaceful city. There were no sounds from the riots. It was only Uri ambling toward Alondra and the voices constantly directing her on this path.

Uri rubbed her neck and listened to Alondra as her voice deepened to a growl while speaking.

"Sergeant Uri," Alondra hissed, "we refuse to tolerate this constant struggle between humans and the restoration of Earth! You have failed to show us any desire to work with the caretakers! Now tell me"—Alondra stretched out a hand to the civilians—"is this fight the cause of your kind?"

The leeches slithered to the back of Uri's brain as she tried to conjure up a response that would satisfy Alondra. Static filled Uri's head as she thought, *Not even the leeches will be able to help me.*

A bunch of the civilians yelled at Alondra. A few even tried throwing stones at her, yet they failed to penetrate Alondra's flesh or completely missed Alondra. Alondra's ears twitched, and she whipped her head around at the citizens, unleashing a human scream.

Uri cringed when she heard the leeches screech in response to Alondra's bones slightly cracking from the stones being thrown at her. Uri and Márquez turned around in response to thunderous stomping. Uri made out the silhouettes of Liana and Damek as they too approached Glass City with an intense rage radiating from their beings.

Groups of civilians scrambled for whatever shelter they could find in the city, which was slowly turning into a part of the Wastelands. Some of the civilians threw stones at the caretakers, ignoring the warnings from their fellow civilians.

Alondra let out another humanlike screech. The ground shook as a collection of shrieks rumbled in the distance. Animals and other caretakers could be seen stampeding toward Glass City. Uri heard a screech overhead and looked up to see bats dive for the building. Uri and Márquez ducked to the ground as the bats flew over them.

Uri looked up as one of the bats swiped her up by her shoulders and legs and flew away from the riots. "Oh God!" Uri shrieked. She looked down and watched Glass City shrink as she was carried away.

"I would just go with whatever happens," the voice of Uri's father said. "Besides, these bats belong to Alondra, correct? And you trust Alondra."

"I trusted Alondra to help me locate survivors, not to be picked up and carried to God only knows where!" Uri shouted.

The bats chirped at each other and changed the direction of their flight. They flew in a half circle toward what appeared to be a scrapyard. The bat lowered Uri to the ground and dropped her on her side.

Uri watched as the bats flew off toward Glass City again. She scratched her head as she stood up and sighed. She recognized the main entrance of the scrapyard where she once took refuge. The grotesque garbage remained, the towering piles taunting Uri because she had lost track of her survivors and almost all of her equipment.

"Great," she hissed. "Back to square one."

CHAPTER 23

U ri hunted through the piles of garbage that she suspected were places where the bats would drop survivors. She searched through the piles that appeared caved in and surrounded by loose trash.

The leeches let out their clicking noises. Uri ignored them and used her free will to dig through the garbage while she could. The rust from dew-laced metal and ash coated Uri's mud-stained hands and seeped into her cuts, causing the leeches to grow hysterical.

"What are you doing?" one leech hissed and pulled Uri back from the garbage. "You know that Alondra's bats wouldn't just drop humans anywhere."

The leeches forced Uri's feet to slide through the dirt and turn toward a pile of cans. They then brought Uri's hands forward, and she began pulling handfuls of cans away from the pile.

The leeches hummed and pulled Uri back to her feet, "Not there!" they sang and dragged Uri to a pile of papers. The leeches hummed again before shrieking, "Not there either!" They pulled Uri to a pile of cotton clothing.

"Do you know if there are even survivors in this

scrapyard?" Uri asked as she was whisked away to a pile of rusted scrap metal. She hesitated over a pile of cardboard that appeared to have been caved in from someone's fall.

"We don't even know if the bats will remember to return to the scrapyard"—the leeches giggled—"much less if Alondra is planning to look for you."

Uri rubbed her head as the leeches broke out into hysterical laughter. Their laughing changed to static and eventually dropped to whispers. Uri felt her thoughts slowly drift back to her own mind. She gently moved her fingers and groaned at how cramped her body felt. Her vision changed to gray again.

The monochromatic scene of the scrapyard slowly took Uri back to a previous vision in which she was standing outside of the apartment complex. This time Uri was staring down at the garbage inside the trash cans that she assumed represented the caretakers. She looked down at a fur coat. Colorless gems glistened in the oddly bright moonlight.

Uri stopped by a black dog curled up; a large bump was moving beneath its flesh. Her eyes followed the bump as it inched toward a hole that had been eaten out of the dog's stomach. A plump red and black leech squirmed out of the dog's wound and fell onto the alleyway's concrete. It let out a scream that sounded similar to the noise of a rioting crowd as it lay excreting purple slime.

"I would back away slowly if I were you," one voice giggled, "unless you want twice as many voices swarming inside of your head."

Uri followed the voice's order and continued through the city. The voices chuckled and threw themselves against Uri's frontal lobe. She lost her balance and stretched out her arm to lean against one of the apartment buildings. Her hand pushed against the concrete wall, and it broke off into crumpled pieces of paper. The buildings twisted and curled downward into piles of garbage. The concrete sidewalk and asphalt road crumbled into desert sand. The dark blue night sky turned to gray clouds. Despite the stormy appearance, there was no wind, no rain, and no thunder or lightning.

"Don't worry," the voices gently sang. "This vision will not be as horrible as the vision of the city."

"I prefer the city as opposed to bleeding landscape colors and pitch-black voids," Uri said with a low hiss.

The voices murmured among themselves. The piles of garbage formed back into the city setting. This time, some of the smaller piles changed into cars, people, and domestic animals.

"What is all of this?" Uri asked.

"You said you wanted the city mirage," the voices hissed. "Don't tell us you've changed your mind."

"I don't care what mirage you set up for me. I just want to be able to locate survivors if there are any."

Uri ceased walking in hopes of hearing the voices' response. She listened to the voices murmur among themselves, and then they became silent. She could only hear the sound of the breeze and the echoing noise of the city. Uri walked through a crowd of people. She bumped into a few of them, yet no one noticed her.

"How am I supposed to find survivors in this mirage?"

Uri waited for the voices' response but heard nothing from them. A short man who looked similar to Quick walked directly into Uri. As she pushed the man back, he crumbled into a pile of sand.

"Just poke at everyone until they don't turn into sand," the voices stated.

"No!" Uri shouted. She looked around hoping she had not caused a scene. Everyone appeared to go on their way without acknowledging her.

Uri turned to a nearby two-story building that was completely constructed of glass. "There's no way." Uri pressed her fingers against the revolving glass door. The entire building quietly crumbled into a pile of sand, as the voices said.

Uri looked around. No one appeared to notice the building crumbling to sand.

She moved on to the next building. The voices pushed against Uri's frontal lobe while chanting, "Go down there!" She turned down an alleyway lined with dumpsters and metal trash cans. She pulled off the lid of the first trash can. Inside were piles of dead animals. Uri held her breath as she searched through the pile; however, she was only able to dig up small domestic animals.

Uri slammed the lid back down and moved on to the next trash can. This one held the same freshly clipped weeds as the trash can from Uri's previous vision. Uri stared at the weeds that moved subtly as though they were knitting themselves together. Five small slits formed in the weeds resembling a human face. Two small slits opened up into two empty sockets, and Uri quickly put the lid back on the trash can.

Uri then turned to the fur coat covered in gems. Small bumps traveled beneath the coat until two leeches squirmed out from under the right sleeve.

"This had better be good," she muttered.

Uri crept down the alleyway, waiting for something to jump out and chase her. She stopped at the last dumpster and saw someone she assumed was Chávez, unconscious and propped up against the wall.

The concrete and glass buildings of the city turned back into piles of garbage. The people, vehicles, and domestic animals crumbled into desert sand as the voices pulled Uri back. She stared at Chávez as piles of trash formed around his unconscious body.

As the voices reverted back to their distant clicking, Uri tried to help Chávez. She pushed bags of broken bottles and open aluminum cans off of his body.

Uri listened as the voices muttered while she pulled Chávez out of the pile. She fell back, and Chávez fell on her without waking up. The mountain of bottles and cans tumbled down, thickening the river of trash beneath it.

Uri looked down at Chávez. "How long has he been here?" she wondered as she tried to feel his pulse. She had no means of communication, fast transportation, or medical equipment.

The voices let out their clicking noises again. "Now

what?" they asked.

Uri bent down and lifted Chávez. "He is still breathing. He probably just passed out from being carried by the bats."

"Blame the bats!" the voices cried. "Alondra would not be too fond of that."

"Alondra," Uri whispered as she began walking, balancing Chávez in her arms. Her eyes widened as she almost dropped him. "Oh God, the caretakers will kill the survivors."

"Why?" the voices asked.

"I mean, they..." Uri hesitated as she readjusted Chávez in her arms. "Just seeing how angry they were when they left the Meeting Grounds."

"We can always figure something out together," the voices answered. "The perfect combination: the only human the caretakers trust and one of Alondra's own creations."

"Well, what do you think the caretakers will do after I return to them? Already Quick stole gems from Damek, and Liana is worried about her dying plants because she chose to sleep instead of taking care of the problem."

Uri paused in thought. "Alondra is currently the only one who shows some support for allowing humans back on Earth. Unfortunately, it's only because she wants assistance with her animals."

"But you have Alondra's support," the voices hissed. "Isn't that enough?"

"The caretakers will still want to hold a meeting in order to make decisions," Uri growled, "and knowing Alondra, she will at least attempt to back up my proposition until a human kills one of her animals."

Uri paused when the voices' clicking noises started up again. The voices died down, allowing Uri to finish. "Even then, they will end up arguing about the same crap they brought up at their last meeting."

"Yes," the voices responded flatly to Uri's thought. "So about those caretakers..."

"Forget it." Uri shrugged. "They're not that smart, and I doubt that they would help me."

The voices laughed and whispered. Uri twitched as one bloated leech struggled to slither into her ear canal. The leech grunted as if it were caught on something and was now attempting to pull itself loose. Uri scratched her ear, and one of the leeches screeched. She yelped as a set of fangs sunk into her outer ear.

"Do not try to remove us while we're thinking!" the bloated leech barked and bit down harder on her ear.

Uri hissed in pain, and she pushed her hand into her forehead. She looked over to see the purple slime drip onto her shoulder as the voices made their clicking noises.

"Ah! I've got an idea," a leech with Uri's voice piped up.

"A little late for that, wouldn't you say?" Uri hissed as she set Chávez on a mattress. She pushed her fingers into her temples to see if the pressure would help the leeches. She felt the leeches squirm for a bit until one of them jerked its body.

"You know three of the caretakers personally, correct?" the leech hummed.

"Yeah," Uri said cautiously.

She rubbed her ear again as she felt the bloated leech bite down harder on her concha. Uri wearily watched as blood and slime dripped down her shoulder. She grew dizzy as she tried to focus on what the leeches had to say.

"Well, it's obvious that the other caretakers are still out there," the leech with Uri's voice said. "We'll help you find those caretakers, as well as other survivors. We'll strike a different deal with them than you did with Alondra, and those caretakers will decide that humans should be allowed to roam Earth again. It will be like nothing ever happened."

"Sounds impossible," Uri said, "and complicated." She felt the bloated leech loosen its bite a little, relieving some of her pain.

"But it's not," the bloated leech said. "Here, we'll show you."

The bloated leech crawled deeper into Uri's ear canal and said, "First leave the scrapyard; once you're out, we'll take over from there."

"This had better be good," Uri hissed.

The scrapyard morphed into the void. A dirt path formed beneath Uri's feet, and the leeches guided her forward. She looked to the horizon where the path and the void met and continued walking. She looked behind her, watching as shadows of strange animals formed along the path, and quickly turned her head back.

The animals crept alongside in the same motion as Benjamin moved in the shadows, giving an eerie mood to the void. Uri turned to her left, and the animals formed a wall with their bodies. She turned to her right where the path continued. She walked farther down the path until she came to another fork. The shadowy animals formed a wall on the right side, forcing Uri to take the left path. She shifted to the left one more time as the animals formed into more walls around her.

"Wait, Sergeant Uri," the voices said. "You have arrived."

The void cleared, and Uri saw a pile of garbage that grew taller and spread outward. The sky changed to a pink-purple gradient building that spread outward. The building appeared to be a two-story house with a large glass dome and overgrown plant life. The glass windows were broken, and the paint had chipped off in large chunks. Uri carefully stepped forward, watching for any animals or other creatures that looked as though they had taken over the building.

The voices caused her feet to slide forward and pulled her into the entryway of the building.

CHAPTER 24

The leeches forcefully caused Uri's head to shake as they screeched, and she clasped her hands over her ears. The scene of the mansion switched from blurry to clear and back to blurry again. A mix of chattering, screaming, and whispering collided as the leeches argued.

"You should have provided Sergeant Uri with better directions!" one leech hissed.

"No!" a second leech responded harshly. "It was your job to guide her feet, and you just led her to that insane caretaker who decided to remove the first leech from Uri's ear."

"I did my absolute best!" the first leech snapped back. "It was you who provided Uri with confusing directions and vague ideas!"

The leeches' thick, slimy bodies slid toward the entrance of Uri's ear canal as their arguing grew louder. Uri's fingers twitched and her joints popped as she stretched out her arm, acknowledging her strength returning. She reached into her ear, feeling for the end of one of the leeches and pulled. The leeches' screams grew shrill as they attempted to dig themselves deeper into Uri's ear canal. Uri hooked her index finger around one of the leeches and ripped it directly out of her ear. She screeched in response as her ear throbbed from the overly nourished leeches gasping and squirming toward the outside.

She felt more slime pool up at the entrance of her ear. Thousands of tiny leeches spilled onto the broken tiles of the mansion in a puddle of caramel ear wax and cherry-syrup blood with the remaining purple slime. Uri felt one more ball of slime slide toward the entrance of her ear canal. A large, overnourished leech slid forward. It attempted to attach itself to the flesh of Uri's ear and strained to pull itself back into her ear. Uri locked her fingers onto the leech's tail and pulled. She felt the leech slide out farther and wrapped her fingers around it until the leech choked. Uri felt the leech cease fighting and pulled the rest of it out. More purple slime, blood, and ear wax dripped from her ear, carrying more of the tiny leeches with the flow.

As the last of the slime came out, Uri's sight returned to reality. The mansion surrounded by the city shifted back into the scrapyard. The monochromatic color gave way to the scene's natural colors. Layers of sand formed around the scrapyard from previous sandstorms.

The collision of pastel rainbows from the theme park and industrial grays and reds from the scrapyard grew intense in the sunlight. The sand gained its natural light brown color as it was tossed into the desert wind that curled around the scrapyard's metals, creating eerie whistles and creaks.

Uri looked up to see a plump, six-inch-long, red and

black leech wrap its body around a piece of broken glass and squirm and screech in agony as purple slime spilled out of its body. More screeches echoed throughout the different sections of the scrapyard in response to the one leech. Uri hopped over a fallen wicker swing and ran into the destroyed theme park, looking back to see a red and black leech slither after her. She could hear it pant heavily as it attempted to catch up to her. The leech cried out, "Sergeant Uri! Where are you going?"

Uri picked up Chávez, jumped a turnstile, and ran through the ticket booth attached to the Lost Children's Center. The ceiling of the Lost Children's Center had caved in from broken chunks of Uri's previous base and the theme park's equipment falling through the ceiling.

Uri propped up Chávez at an office desk inside the room and walked into the break room. She leaned against the counter, rapidly tapping her fingers against the worn plywood countertop. She remained clueless about whether or not one of the caretakers would come for her or if they would have a sudden urge to kill her and Chávez. Uri lowered her head to the countertop and murmured to herself.

"I could retrace my steps back to Alondra's territory," Uri said. She perked up at the idea, hoping that as long as she remained with Chávez, Alondra would not harm him. "Then again, Alondra could still be tearing down Glass City."

"Who...is Alondra?"

Uri flinched and looked down to see Chávez slowly straighten his back. Chávez pulled in both of his legs and scrunched his body into a ball.

"Who are you, and why are you talking to yourself?" he murmured.

Before Uri could respond, she heard a short laugh come from him. "Wait, I remember who you are."

Chávez lifted his head, revealing bloodshot eyes surrounded by dark circles. He stood up and leaned against the office wall. He scratched his ear, and tiny dark red leeches slipped out. Uri guessed that Chávez happened to scratch the leeches out before they could grow older and take control of his body.

"You were that soldier I talked to behind the perimeter of the academy," Chávez said. He yawned before speaking again. "It looks like those bats were merciful to you too."

"Yeah, they were," Uri said and smiled. She hesitated, wondering whether or not to explain the caretakers to him.

Chávez grunted as he readjusted his posture. He appeared to have not had a cushioned landing when the bats dropped him in the scrapyard. "Have you seen anyone else yet?" he asked.

Uri's expression went blank. She assumed that Chávez would be in search of staff and students from the academy when he woke up.

Uri wandered down the hallway. She wouldn't be able to contact LIES or Shamayim's government. Uri would either need to wait or to travel for help with Chávez, and even Shamayim's government would leave Uri out for returning with only one survivor. She wandered through the halls in search of anything valuable that was left behind by survivors or before the Mysterious War.

The rooms had been stripped of their contents. Pictures were torn off the wall in the Missing Children's Room. The offices were completely cleaned out of their supplies, including desks and chairs. Uri slowly made her way back to where she left Chávez. He was now sitting on the ground in the same place, giving Uri more time to attempt to contact Shamayim without any disruptions.

"Wait!" Uri groaned. "My communicator died, and I threw it in that swamp."

Aggravation built up inside of Uri at this realization. She dragged her feet back to the entrance of the ticket booth, attempting to conjure up a way to get in touch with Shamayim. She leaned her back against the hallway's wall and slid down until she was sitting on the ground.

Outside, the sound of loud footsteps could be heard approaching the theme park. Uri looked out the entrance of the ticket booth. From a distance, she could see Damek's long streamer-like fur was blowing in the wind.

Uri gritted her teeth as she recognized Damek. She grew fearful and agitated as she imagined what he would say to her.

Damek let out an aggrieved sigh as he pushed the burnt remains of the theme park's attractions aside. He appeared to be exhausted from tending to his gem forest, supplying the other caretakers' needs, and caring for the earth's soils. His back was hunched up to his shoulders, and his head remained tilted down as if he was more focused on his large gait tossing up sand and garbage rather than how quickly he approached Uri.

"Crap," Uri muttered, "why is Damek here? Did he get injured? Did Alondra or another caretaker get injured or killed? Has Damek's gem forest been destroyed? Did another caretaker's territory get destroyed? Will Damek blame me for whoever's death was caused or whose territory was destroyed? Oh God, he could only bring bad news."

Uri shivered and grew tense as strands of Damek's fur extended and wrapped around her body. Uri struggled as Damek lifted her up; however, with each movement she made, he only tightened his grasp. Uri felt his body shake slightly after she was stopped at his eye level. The single glowing orb in the center of his face turned red, and his shorter strands of fur stood up as if held by static from a balloon.

A low growl escaped from Damek's mouth. "So, Davida Uri, now that you have your survivors, will you finally run back to wherever you came from and leave us alone to tend to Earth?"

"Didn't Alondra say that the other humans and I could stay and help?" Uri snapped. "Is she not the leader of the caretakers?"

Damek lowered his head closer to Uri's. "I'm willing to listen to Alondra, but when the fate of our world comes down to being rescued by the very monsters that turned our creations against us, I will not tolerate it; also, Alondra is not the leader of the caretakers; as a matter of fact, we do not have a leader."

"The fate of your world?" Uri spoke firmly. "We did not cause the destruction of Earth; it was those strange Hawkins creatures and their leeches."

Damek's hair wrapped around Uri, and he guided her deeper into the ruins of the amusement park. Uri watched as his hair ran along the surfaces while his red orb grew darker. "Originally," he said through clinched teeth, "it was Alondra who created those leeches. She managed to cut off their food supply in order to make them vegetarians, so they needed something else to eat. As for the Hawkinses, I still don't know what they are, unless they are some pathetic excuses for caretakers."

Uri cocked her head. "Aren't they also human? They claimed to be; they were just under the leeches' control."

Damek turned his head to Uri. The hair on his back stood up again. "Be very careful if you decide to share that with Alondra."

Damek brushed piles of gravel off of a caved-in trailer. He picked up one of the pieces and gently placed it into the broken concrete ground. He took up another piece and added it to the corner. When he tried a third piece, he struggled as he rotated and moved pieces of gravel around the hole.

Uri only stared. Her eyelids lowered in sadness as she watched Damek constantly struggle.

"Damek," she said, "I know that you want to care for the minerals of Earth, but is that really necessary?"

He ignored Uri and continued to piece the concrete back together as if he were solving a tiling puzzle. Damek repeatedly rotated and crammed the pieces into the hole in the ground. Some of the concrete was missing pieces, or the smaller pieces required had crumbled into dust.

"I care for every inch of Earth," Damek exclaimed. "That includes asphalt and concrete. Now leave me alone; I must fix this."

Uri looked on sadly at Damek's pointless task. "How can Damek be so stuck on one thing that it stops him from moving on?" Uri asked herself.

"I...I can," Uri stuttered as she felt Damek's fur tighten around her torso. She took a deep breath and blinked, this time maintaining her focus on his burning red orb instead of his tentacles that would snap Uri in half. "I can explain," she said firmly. "The Hawkinses are the ones who destroyed your territories; however, Alondra arrived at their city to wipe them out."

Damek's fur lay flat against his body as if he were satisfied with Uri's response. He then turned away from her to finish rearranging the chunks of broken concrete. "Good," he said, "now will you leave us alone and return to your Shamayim or paradise or whatever you call it?"

"No," Uri responded boldly.

Uri felt the vibrations on the ground as Damek growled, causing the remains of the theme park to shake. She looked into his red orb as he continued.

"I want humans to be able to roam freely on Earth because Alondra said she would allow it." Uri narrowed her eyes. "Why is she not your leader? She tends to be the only caretaker who makes any sense."

"Alondra is not the leader of the caretakers!" Damek lashed out. "If you haven't noticed, and I can tell you haven't, Alondra is easily misled, dependent on her own emotions, and only lives for her animals. She is everything that I am not!"

An earthquake rolled through, followed by the crashing of the titanium roller coaster in the distance. A sandstorm blew through the scrapyard, coating Damek's fur. Sweat poured off of his fur turning the dirt in his fur to mud.

"Are you kidding me?" Uri smirked and shook her head.

"Is there something you find humorous, Davida?" Damek leaned over her. His orb turned to a darker shade of red.

Uri reconsidered her physical appearance and quickly snapped back into her more serious self. "Damek," she said, "I can see you're upset about the destruction of the world; however, could you just talk to Liana or the other caretakers? Or have you tried talking to Alondra?"

Damek ran his paws through his hair. Large drops of sweat rolled off of his body. He turned away from Uri and looked down at the ground, focusing on realigning pieces of concrete, possibly as a way to get out of answering her.

"Can you at least reconsider talking to Alondra?" Uri asked.

Damek turned his head, allowing his fur strands to push Uri back. His red orb changed to a soothing blue as he moved on to filling a hole with sand. "I may have underestimated you, Dav...Uri."

Uri perked up. "Well, that's a first. Why are you suddenly behaving so formal?"

"I will," Damek hesitated, "have to agree with Alondra. It's apparent you could be of some value to us, which would give me a reason to talk to her."

Uri cocked her head as Damek motioned for her to follow. He stopped Uri abruptly and leaned into her face. "But understand, I still hate you and your kind."

Uri nodded and nervously responded, "I understand."

"Come with me. I know where you can find the survivors your world leaders seek."

CHAPTER 25

Damek looked up toward the ticket booth behind Uri. She followed Damek's orb and saw Chávez leaning against the frame of the entrance after he tripped on the loose floor tiles. Chávez wearily brought his hands over his eyes to block out the desert sunlight, and Uri rushed over to meet him. She pushed Chávez forward while she said, "There is someone here who will help us. It is important that you show him respect."

"Okay," Chávez muttered, still rubbing his eyes. "Is it one of the academy's instructors?" Chávez pulled his hands away, and his eyes widened as he tilted his head upward at Damek. He screamed and backed up into the wall of the ticket booth. Uri looked at Damek, whose orb turned dark red again. Uri hurried to calm Chávez down while studying any disappointment in Damek's body language.

Damek's red orb turned to multicolors as he looked over Chávez. He wrapped his strands of fur around the boy's small frame while a few of his strands pushed back Uri.

Chávez screamed louder and attempted to fight his way through the fur, yet Damek remained calm and lifted him up. Chávez bit and scratched at Damek's appendages.

Uri gasped and yelled at Chávez while she waited anxiously for Damek's reaction. "Remain calm, Chávez!"

Chávez breathed heavily, still squirming in Damek's grasp. Damek brought him closer to his orb and carefully looked him over. Chávez leaned back to the edge of Damek's hand. Damek's posture straightened out and his orb changed to a light blue.

"Excellent!" Damek exclaimed. "You do have a survivor. You do give Alondra a reason to be proud of you. Now come; I'll lead you to your workplace."

Damek gently placed Chávez down and walked away from the ticket booth. His fur gently pulled on Uri and Chávez, guiding them forward.

Uri pushed Chávez along, feeling him drag his feet in the sand.

Chávez then grabbed Uri and pulled her in front of him. "What the hell are you doing?" he hissed.

"I said that Damek would help us," Uri said. She walked around Chávez and proceeded to follow Damek before she felt Chávez tug her back by her shoulder.

"Yeah, a human Damek," Chávez said, strongly emphasizing the word "human." "Not something that looks like a reject from a plush toy factory."

Chávez shuddered and crouched behind Uri when Damek whipped his head toward them. His orb turned to a dark red.

Uri held up her hands, motioning for Damek to wait. "Please, do not hurt him," she whispered.

Damek grunted in response and continued walking through the Wastelands. "He's still disrespectful," he mumbled.

Damek ambled onward while Uri pushed Chávez. Eventually, the group reached the highway, and Damek followed the road toward the off-ramp. He looked down to see the heels of Chávez's shoes scrape along the asphalt. Uri pushed him up until she got him to stand straight. She looked up to Damek who kept walking and then leaned next to Chávez's ear.

"Keep walking, Chávez," Uri murmured. "As long as you are respectful to Damek, he will not hurt you."

Chávez nodded and followed while maintaining a slow pace. Uri looked back and frowned as she watched him back up and follow the two at a distance of ten feet. Uri ran up to Damek's side. He looked down at Uri and spoke in a deep gravelly voice. "You may speak, Uri."

"This place you scouted out, Damek," Uri said, "what's it like?"

Damek's orb turned a bright orange, and his gravelly voice grew bold and cheerful. "I'm glad you asked!" he said. "It's a large city that should fit all of your kind, and it's far away from all of the caretakers' territories."

"What else can you tell me about it?" Uri asked.

"It's the most perfect place that I've found, no doubt," Damek boasted. "None of the other caretakers know about it yet; however, I know they will love it too."

Uri glanced over at Chávez, whose eyes looked up at

Damek in hesitation. Damek advanced toward the destination with a confident appearance. He led her and Chávez onto a highway that led to a collection of skyscrapers about fifty miles away. Uri recognized the city as the place where the leeches first took her. The bright sun splashed on the city

She could hear gasps and screams. Eventually, Uri made out short phrases from the city.

"Everyone quiet!" one survivor shouted. "It has returned."

"Oh God," another survivor exclaimed. "Why is it keeping us here?"

Damek outstretched his arms. "These are your survivors," he said. "Allow your leaders to join your new territory and leave us alone."

Uri stared at the crowd until she recognized everyone's face. The crowd of survivors only consisted of the staff and students from the academy, including Principal Smith and Vice Principal Davis. They all appeared to be unharmed, aside from the tears on their shirts' shoulders where Alondra's bats had carried them. She gritted her teeth when she caught Márquez glaring at her from the front.

"Damek, where are the other survivors?" Uri asked hesitantly.

"These are the survivors!" Damek said proudly. "I found them all inside some barricaded city. At least they weren't hostile."

Uri looked over at Chávez.

"He's a mass of sentient hair," Chávez whispered. "Of course they would be afraid."

Uri and Chávez turned at the sound of cars pulling up to the city. The world leaders of Shamayim were exiting their vehicles while staring at Damek. Damek stood still, and his orb turned to a soothing light blue. His fur was wrapped back against his body to keep from touching the world leaders and startling them.

Uri spoke calmly to each survivor, explaining the situation. Some quietly nodded; others looked around frantically. Uri then approached the world leaders with the same explanation.

"Sergeant Uri."

Uri saw one of the world leaders approach her, while still keeping an eye on Damek's strands of fur.

"We need to speak to you," the leader stuttered. She tried to remain as professional as she could. "You've helped us find and relocate survivors. Well done."

Uri looked at Damek, whose orb turned to lavender as he grew captivated by the survivors. She watched as he began to introduce himself, causing a minor earthquake. People either remained still or ran for shelter. Uri heard a minor amount of disapproval in Damek's voice as he explained the caretakers' needs and plans for Earth.

The survivors huddled nervously together in response to Damek's powerful voice. Some even backed away, still in fear of his physical appearance. They remained silent, but a few survivors gently nodded or even responded with "yes" or "no" whenever Damek made a statement or asked a question.

"Come, Sergeant." The world leader guided Uri away during Damek's introduction. "I and the rest of the world leaders need to speak..."

Uri's eyes bulged as she was pulled away from the leader and turned around. She took a deep breath as she faced Márquez's glare.

"Oh no," Márquez growled, shaking his finger at Uri. "The entire academy is...well, God only knows what happened to it! We may have some staff and students, but I'm still holding you accountable for any damages or casualties that happened to the other staff and students, as well as the entire facility!"

The nearby survivors gasped and looked at each other. They began whispering about Márquez's words, debating what was true or false.

The world leader looked at Uri with piercing eyes. "Sergeant," he spoke earnestly, "what does this man mean by 'damages or casualties'?"

"Considering that Uri saved under one-third of the academy," Márquez continued.

Uri looked back at the crowd. She counted the students and staff of the academy again and again—first by ones, then by twos—while everyone stared back hesitantly. She realized that a large group of the survivors from the academy were absent.

No, that can't be true, she thought as she held up her

trembling finger to count one more time.

The leaders of Shamayim gasped and exchanged glances at each other.

Uri felt her body tremble.

"No," she said, "Alondra's bats wouldn't hurt anyone unless..."

"Unless what?" one of the world leaders hissed.

Uri saw Damek turning in her direction. His orb was now a dark green as if puzzled by the situation. Uri was now worried about losing favor with Alondra after all the support she gave her. All it would take was one automatic bad action from one of the survivors, and Damek would start another fight with Alondra over allowing humans to expand to Shamayim.

"Unless Alondra commanded them to, but she would never do that," Uri said quickly. "The caretakers are here to help us, and we'll help them restore Earth. That way everyone can live comfortably here."

"Comfortably?" Damek said. His orb now turned red as he leaned into Uri's face. His fiery ash breath caused Uri to drip steaming sweat.

"Comfortably together," Uri added. She listened as Damek's breathing grew heavy, causing the ground to gently shake beneath her feet. She even felt Márquez's burning glare.

"Together?" one survivor shouted. "What makes you think I would want to get along with that giant mop?" She pointed at Damek.

"We are the reason Earth remains!" Damek said.

The woman responded with a smirk.

"If anything," Damek continued, "we, the caretakers, would suggest that you must stay out of our way while we restore Earth for you now."

"Well, who were you restoring Earth for in the first place?" a middle-aged man shouted from the center of the crowd.

The crowd followed the man's response, also shouting at Damek, "Yeah! Why are you the one responsible for restoring the Earth?"

Damek's fur rose up on his back. His orb grew redder with each shout from the crowd.

"Not only that, but what about our academy?" a teenager shouted, followed by the crowd asking the same question.

"Apparently," Damek said, raising his voice, "I am unable to meet everyone's unreasonable needs!"

"Unreasonable!" some people scoffed.

"Everyone, please!" Uri begged. "Try to focus."

"On what?" Another one of the world leaders lashed out. "Why should we listen to you if you help monsters that hate our kind?"

"We are not monsters!" Damek yelled.

"Well, you're certainly not human!" a world leader shouted with a scowl on his face.

Damek turned back to Uri. The ground shook even more until plants made of cinnabar sprouted from the ground, "I supported you!" Damek shouted. "I gave you a second chance, and this is what I get in return?"

"Yeah!" the crowd shouted, "blame the Sergeant!"

Uri backed up as the crowd's demand grew louder. "Exile her! Kill her! Do whatever it takes to keep the peace!"

"Wait! You don't understand!" Uri shouted.

"Oh, we understand plenty," the world leader said through clenched teeth. "Now get out!"

The crowd gathered around Uri. With angry faces, they closed in on her. Uri felt her feet rise off the ground as she was lifted up over the people's heads while they chanted, "Exile Sergeant Uri!"

Uri kicked and squirmed as her body was carried backward. She tried screaming for Damek. She watched as Damek returned to the argument that had sparked between Uri and the world leaders.

"Damek, no!" Uri called out as she was tossed just outside the city.

She looked up to see the crowd form a barrier around the city with their backs facing her. She ran up to the crowd in an attempt to push her way through. The crowd remained tightly knit together, continuing their riot against Damek, as Uri tried to get through them.

Uri backed up as the crowd and Damek spouted profanities at each other. She turned away as Damek shouted another lecture while causing crystal-like growths to sprout from the ground. The crystal grew taller until the entire city of Shamayim was surrounded by a barrier of raw diamond.

Uri pounded her fist against the raw diamond barricade.

Screams followed Damek's commands, which were funneled out from the hole in the top of the barricade. Uri gripped onto the barricade and pulled herself up. She managed to get both feet up onto the diamond and climb about three feet before the raw diamond turned into cut diamond, and she slid to the ground.

Uri could only imagine what Damek was doing to the survivors as she ran around the barrier in search of any openings to get back into Shamayim.

A part of the barrier lowered a little. Uri watched as Damek's arm extended over the barrier and gently touched the ground. Uri spotted something moving beneath the fur and hurried to push the fur out of her way until human hands shot out and grabbed the collar of her jacket. Uri struggled, squeezing the arm in an attempt to get the attacker to let go. Damek pulled his fur away from the arm, revealing more of the person who was choking Uri. Uri saw Chávez still holding his hands around her neck with a furious scowl on his face.

"Chávez!" Uri gasped, still struggling to pry his hands off of her throat. "Are you and Márquez related or what? Why do you both hate me?"

Chávez frowned and let go of Uri's throat. He walked away from her, kicking up the sand in his path.

"Where are you going?" Uri asked.

Chávez turned with a forced smile of agitation. "Where could I be going?" His voice grew higher. "I'm trying to get as far away from you as possible, seeing how whenever I'm around you, my entire life gets screwed up!"

Uri squinted and clenched her teeth as Chávez walked away from Shamayim, his body becoming a silhouette as he moved farther into the desert.

"How could I possibly be the reason that your entire life is ruined?" Uri shouted.

"Let me think!" Chávez laughed impatiently. "You show up at my school—a school, mind you, where I actually had a chance to have a successful future—and then the bats that belong to this creature, you claim to know, take me away from my potential future. Your bats took me into the wilderness, separated me from my instructors, and I survived, until I was kidnapped by those Hawkins creatures that are possessed by some worm!"

"A leech," Uri corrected.

Chávez shot Uri a glare.

Uri sighed as she listened to Chávez go on about his predicament.

"And then I was stuck with those Hawkins monsters because those bats dropped me off!"

As Uri took a deep breath, Chávez interjected, "Wait a minute, how do you know about the leeches?"

"The leeches were an attempt, by one of the caretakers, to make all animals vegetarians," Uri said. "Of course, one of the leeches was overlooked, and instead, it decided to enter my brain and control my thoughts. When I started communicating with the leeches, I managed to reach a compromise with them, and they somewhat, assisted me on my mission to search for the survivors. But, as I traveled, I found out that other creatures occupied Earth. Although, I do not know how they got here, other than they've told me time and again, that they've always been here on Earth."

Chávez stared at Uri with his mouth agape, ready to ask questions. "Will that furry monster kill everyone in Shamayim?" Chávez asked.

"I doubt it," Uri scoffed. "Damek would never kill a crowd of humans, especially without Alondra knowing. She's a caretaker for animal life and now cares for humans in the same way."

"So," Chávez eyed Uri carefully, "the giant furry monster who calls himself Damek, there are others like him?"

"Yes," Uri said. "They are called caretakers and have taken domain over the Earth. It is the same with the Hawkins family."

Uri looked over at Chávez again. He appeared completely confused by her explanation. "I know," she said. "I have no explanation for them either."

Chávez nodded, the confused expression still on his face. Uri simply walked forward without acknowledging his confusion.

"So, that furry thing..."

"Damek," Uri said, "his name is Damek."

"Damek," Chávez murmured. "Damek is someone who wants you to do what exactly?"

"The same mission the world leaders gave me," Uri said. "They were the people you met that run Shamayim, the city you were brought to by the bats."

"So, what did Mr. Márquez say about finding the students?" Chávez asked.

Uri looked at him, his face a mixture of confusion and panic.

"Unfortunately," Uri hesitated, "Márquez claims that Damek failed to find all of the staff and students from the academy, so I'm being sent out to find the rest of them."

Uri was unsure how to explain Alondra's bats, which were picking up the members of the academy. Uri recalled that Chávez was taken away from the academy by Alondra's bats, too. She could only assume that the bats were simply doing what they were meant to do, and the academy happened to get caught up in their daily routine. Uri knew that Alondra would still want to defend her animals, but at the same time she would look after the humans because they were one of the species she was meant to care for.

Uri felt something squirm across her brain. She grasped her head, and a collection of whispers echoed through her mind as the world around her turned into neon colors. She looked over to see Chávez turn into a blur of blues and purples.

"Hello, Sergeant!" the voices greeted Uri in a cheerful manner.

"You again?" Uri pushed her fingers into her ears and began to scratch at the leeches.

"Great to see you again too, Davida." The voice mimicking Uri's father let out an annoyed sigh. "I guess we just grew attached to you."

"Joy," Uri hissed as she scratched her ears harder. "Now is not the best time to let me know that you are still inside my head."

"Well, as we can see, you haven't learned a thing about navigating your new world," the leeches said and laughed. "Therefore, we have decided to remain a part of you for the rest of your life."

Uri pulled her fingers out of her ears as she processed the leeches' words. The scenery turned back into the out-skirts of Shamayim.

"Are you kidding me?" Uri hissed. "I know about the caretakers, the Hawkins family, everything. What else do I need to know to find more survivors?"

"Sergeant Uri?" Chávez squeezed her arm.

She spun around and saw his earnest expression. "Not now, Chávez," she said sternly. "I'm conversing with the leeches."

Chávez responded with a surprised look and backed away from Uri.

She walked away from Chávez and followed the leeches' voices toward the Wastelands. "Okay, leeches, or whatever you call yourselves," Uri hissed.

The leeches mimicked her hiss and pulled Uri into the void, and a dirt path formed in front of her again.

"What are you trying to tell me this time?"

"Well," the leeches replied, laughing, "there are more caretakers, are there not?"

"Yes," Uri said as she thought back to the variety of

caretakers at the meeting. She was curious about what those caretakers were capable of and if they were able to locate the students Márquez claimed to be missing.

"So, where there are caretakers, there are somewhat restored areas of Earth, and where there are restored areas of Earth, there are survivors," the leeches said with a touch of pride before allowing Uri to answer them.

"I see," she said.

"That means we will assist you in finding locations, survivors, and caretakers for the rest of your life," the leeches said. "So, when you do die, we'll just move on to another host or a pool of water, whichever is closest at the time."

"Fair enough," Uri said. "Now, you said you know where the survivors are located?"

"Yes," the leeches responded, "but before we find your survivors, we require food."

"I'll take you back to Alondra," Uri said.

"No, no. Come on!" the leeches whined. "We don't want those berries that Liana created, and we don't want anything that Damek scraped together! Don't you like any good food?"

"We don't have many options for 'good food,'" Uri said. "Get over it."

"Oh, you'd be surprised at what we can find," the leeches said. "We know about places where you can find survivors and we can find food."

Uri thought about the leeches' offer.

"You still don't trust us, do you?" the leeches asked.

"Actually," Uri said, "I believe you will be of value to me."

The leeches became silent.

"I no longer have a navigation device," Uri said, "so I want you to guide me to survivors."

The leeches whispered to each other. Each one formed a different theory regarding Uri's statement.

"She could be a talented liar," one leech said.

"She's probably telling the truth," another responded.

"Make up your minds before I take you to Alondra," Uri said.

The leeches gasped. "No, no, no! You can't just dump us on Alondra. What will she say when she finds out that you refuse to care for us, a precious gift to this world?"

"She'll take you in and provide for you," Uri said. "Or you can cooperate with me and help me find the remaining survivors."

The leeches sighed collectively, sounding similar to the roar of a crowd. The whispering then grew quieter as they talked to each other.

Uri tried to listen to what the leeches were saying, but she could only hear the sound of their static-like whispers.

"Very well," Uri said, "we're going to see Alondra."

"Okay, okay, we've made a decision!" the leeches wailed. "As long as you help us find food, we will help you find survivors."

Uri, venting her frustration with the leeches, commanded them, "start walking!" And they guided her toward the mirage of a new city.

CPSIA information can be obtained
at www.ICGtesting.com
Printed in the USA
JSHW021515150723
44805JS00002B/107